Y0-BWY-276

The Remains of River Names

The Remains of River Names

MATT BRIGGS

BLACK HERON PRESS
POST OFFICE BOX 95676
SEATTLE, WASHINGTON 98145
HTTP://WWW.MAV.NET/BLACKHERON

Winner of the 1998
King County Arts Commission
Publication Award

Several sections of this book have appeared in the following
magazines: "My Name's Roy" in *The Asylum Monthly* and "Jolly
Rancher" in *The North Atlantic Review.*

ISBN 0-930773-56-X

Black Heron Press
Post Office Box 95676
Seattle, WA 98145
http://www.mav.net/blackheron

To Lisa

I would like to express my gratitude to the King County Arts Commission for their support. Thanks as well to my friends Phoebe Bosché at *The Raven Chronicles* and Skip Pipo, Erika Hanson, and Lisa Purdy, at the Greasy Hussy Research Institute.

Contents

My Name's Roy

Before I shake my older brother Milton awake, I eat all the food, a hard dinner roll and a teaspoon of peanut butter scraped from the bottom of the Adam's jar. I set the empty jar quietly in the trash so I won't wake Milton. He grunts in his sleep and I stop my loud chewing. If he knows that I'm eating the last of the food, he'll seriously beat my butt.

Once the roll drops into my stomach, I start to get really hungry. My teeth hurt. I want to fill my mouth with one of the cabinet door knobs just to have something to chew on until the pain in my stomach goes away.

Milton is four years older than me. He goes to middle school, so I don't see much of him around the house except when he's sick. Sometimes in the morning, Milton wakes up for breakfast and he tells me about the motorbike he's rebuilding in the old shed that used to be a horse stable behind our house. Our place used to be a farmhouse. For a while, our dad grew plants behind the thick door of the root cellar and sold the leaves to people who dropped in. Dad and his friends sat around the kitchen table and talked about music while Dad licked sandwich bags closed. My dad, he really likes music. So does Mom. My parents have a stack of albums they play all the time, The Rolling Stones, Paul Butterfield, Jefferson Airplane, bands like that. When my parents are around, the house fills with music and flat, blue clouds of smoke and people talking about stuff that makes everyone laugh. Once in a while, Mom and Dad don't come home for a few days from the parties at their friends' houses. They sleep over a lot.

This morning, as I walk into the living room rubbing the sleep out of my eyes, I realize the Chevy is gone. I see the clotted and oil-stained gravel where the car normally sits in the driveway. The only car in the driveway is my old Tonka dump truck, its yellow bed filling with rain water.

In the big bedroom, the sheets of my parents' bed lay on the floor. My Mom's old blouses, printed with paisleys, blouses with brown and orange and red stripes, are piled up on the bed. She left her old clothes and took all her new clothes, ones she stitched for herself with her new sewing machine. Even the Singer is gone now. She sewed the clothes for herself with the thin, crinkly, cut-out patterns she kept in the white plastic bag from the Benjamin Franklin Variety Store in Issaquah. She took me there once. While she looked through the rolls of cloth, I stuffed a plastic water pistol into my pocket. Before we left, the manager made Mom pay for the pistol and she needed to use our return bus fare. We waited together in the Pick Axe restaurant for Dad to come and pay the tab and take us home. While we sat there, Mom and I did crossword puzzles and I drank one Coke after another. The waiter kept giving us slices of hot sourdough bread with little squares of butter.

Still chewing on the roll, I search through the back of

the cupboards for some food. At the bottom of a macaroni-and-cheese box, I find some noodles and pretend they're popcorn. Mom and Dad have taken all the good stuff from Milton's and my room, my stuffed animals, my box of plastic army soldiers, my battery-powered tank.

I wait for Milton to wake up or Mom to return. I don't have the TV to watch, so I sit on the sofa and page through Mom's old magazines, ones with photographs of gardens and lawn furniture and orderly living rooms with books in the shelves. Mom has all the magazines like this because sometimes they have hints about sewing clothes or, as she once said, "ways to make this pig sty not so piggie." She has *Better Homes & Gardens*, *Redbook*, *Family Circle*. She has a lot of magazines, and reading them is the only thing I can do while I wait to tell my brother what has happened.

I look for pictures of people that look like Mom and Dad, but I can't find them. In Mom's magazines, families eat outside on picnic tables with red and white checkered tablecloths and paper plates instead of the grooved and glazed ceramic plates that Mom made at the Seattle YMCA. Men don't wear long black pony tails, unless they are in biker costumes. But Dad isn't a biker. He drives a car. But instead of a new, little car he drives a rusted Impala Supersport that's older than Milton.

Mom once got in trouble for trying to buy *People* magazine. She slid the magazine from the rack while Dad, her, and I waited behind a man buying a load of beer and watermelon. "Christ," Dad said. He grabbed Mom by her wrists. He told her in a growling voice, "We don't need that filth in our house. Real people don't really read these things, they just sell plastic stuff to plastic people." Then he shook Mom's wrist and tossed the magazine back into the rack. But next time it was just me and her and she slipped the magazine into her bag.

Inside Mom's magazines, I hope I will find some clue as to what she has done, where she has gone. They have been gone before, but they always leave enough food for us. Mom, and especially Dad, have never been good at telling us what the plans are. Our family just does things. One day we will be living in a house, and the next day we will be on the road toward a new city.

"Christ," Milton says when he wakes up and I tell him that Mom and Dad are gone, gone with everything important, like the TV, the stereo, and the cans of chili Dad brought home for us to eat this week. I smell something on my brother's breath like cigarette smoke. He quickly walks around the house rubbing his armpits and smelling his fingers while he looks at the places where our parents' stuff isn't. "Christ," he says again.

"You know what to do," I tell him. He has to know what to do because I've read all the *Redbooks* I can stand.

When my brother opens the refrigerator door, he leaves it open. That's okay because there isn't anything in it.

"Where did they go?" I ask him. I can feel the cold air of the refrigerator filling the kitchen. If Dad saw Milton, someone would be getting some serious blue bruises.

Milton opens the cupboards looking for the chili that's supposed to be there. He looks at all the stuff that isn't there and he says, "Hell, I don't know."

"You don't know? You're my older brother, you have to know, don't you?"

"Don't 'cha?" he says, mimicking me. "Look, we may sleep in the same room. I may sleep in the bunk below you, but that doesn't mean that I'm really your brother. I'm not related to a freak like you."

I sit down on the edge of the table. "We have the same

mother and the same father. I'm not your half brother. I'm your full brother, the real thing."

"If I'm your brother, where are Mom and Dad?" He ducks out of the kitchen and I close the refrigerator door.

He puts on his work shirt and he walks through the rain to the old stable and starts working on his motorcycle that they haven't taken and I wish they had. Sometimes, when my brother pretends he likes me, he calls me Stickbutt because one time when we went skinny dipping in the Snoqualmie River my legs were so skinny he couldn't look at me. "Get your pants back on and hide your skinny ass," he said.

I sit at the window with a handful of magazines and watch the rain fall and roll down the driveway in a muddy stream. While I sit there watching, a police car pulls into the drive, and a policeman in a black rain coat and a big Smokey the Bear hat walks up to the house. He stops to look at my old Tonka truck. I don't want him to think I've ever played with it. When he sees me looking at him, I wave and I open the door. I can take care of myself. I don't want a policeman to take me to a foster home, to a couple of strangers who'd be jealous of my real mom and dad.

"Hello," he says in a deep voice that sounds just like I thought it would sound.

"Hi," I say and I lean against the door, acting like Milton.

"Your parents around?"

"They just left to get some milk," I say, "and some Cheerios. My brother's here, but he says he's not really my brother and he won't listen to me when I tell him he is."

"Yeah," the policeman says. He tips his hat back and looks up to where my brother works and makes a racket in the shed. "Well, he shouldn't say a thing like that to his own brother."

"No, he shouldn't," I say, "but that's the way he is."

"Mind if I take a look around?" he asks me.

"Help yourself," I say.

He walks through the house. He stands in the root cellar where my dad, just yesterday, had been growing his big green plants. "So this is where your dad had his own little garden," the policeman says. He knocks an almost empty ten gallon drum over, dumping out a handful of potting soil. I wait while the policeman goes and tells Milton that he shouldn't talk to his brother the way he does. Milton doesn't even stop working. He just lays under his motorbike because he's so rude.

The policeman gets back into his police car and he says, "When they come home, why don't you give me a call so we don't have to worry about you." The thick blue carpet and warm odor of coffee make me want to get into the car and just sit in the seat and watch the rain rush down the windowpanes. He rips a yellow-lined piece of paper from his plastic notebook. I hold the paper in my hand. His handwriting is square and huge.

"Thanks," I say.

As the police car pulls away, I fall back onto the wet front steps, breathing in the cold odor of moldy wood and listening to the clash of metal from Milton's work. No one will take me away. I can just wait until my parents come home. When they come home with groceries, I'll eat sandwiches and pizzas until I expand like Jiffy Pop. The house will fill with music and smoke and my parents' friends who laugh so hard they have to cover their mouths with both their hands.

Milton fires his motorbike. The engine buzzes and spits like the starting lawn mower. Milton flexes his muscles while he twists the throttle. He looks at me and bats the hair out of his eyes. He grins and laughs but I can't hear his voice over the roar. Dropping the back wheel to the ground, he jumps on the seat and races down the driveway, past me and away. I fold my hands under my butt, and sit with my legs crossed while I listen to the buzz of the bike fade down the road. I wait for him to come back.

He doesn't come back until much later and, by that time, I've drawn the water for a bath and sat in the water until it grew cold. I found an old pair of scissors and cut out all the pictures of women in the magazines and stacked them according to hair color. The blondes have the largest stack but Mom has brown hair and I find a few women with brown hair and I stack them and pair them with likely men. I can't find any man who looks like my father, with his long black ponytail and bristly beard, among the men in blue suits and yellow polo shirts.

A girl with sort of brown hair comes back with Milton. She sits on the back of Milton's motorbike, has her small white hands folded across his chest. She carries a backpack, Alpine Explorer, the same model Milton and Dad use when they go hiking for a long time. They like the metal frame and dozen pockets because they can carry apples or cassette tapes or Milky Ways. Milton rides the bike up the drive and then they jump from the back. She smiles at me and he smiles at me. "Hey Stickbutt," he says, "this is Annie. She's my girl."

"Hey," Annie says. She holds the straps of the backpack with her hands. She flicks up her chin when she says the word like she's just met me on the street or something. She nods like she wants me to think she's cool.

Milton says, "Hey, Babe, give me that backpack." When he takes her off the bike he kisses her on the lips. As he kisses her she closes her eyes and leans back. He kisses her and then he does something gross. He puts his tongue in her mouth.

"Why are you doing that, Milton?" I ask.

He says, "Stop looking, Perve, and take this inside." He tosses me the backpack. It's light. When I take it inside, I find wrinkled shirts, jeans, and an army surplus rain coat stuffed into the main pocket. She has a book, *Hollywood Wives*, by Jackie Collins. I sit on the sofa with the book. Someone has written in loopy handwriting on the inside cover, "To lovely Ann for her fourteenth Birthday."

"You like my book?"

"It fell out of your backpack," I say as I push her clothes back inside the flap.

"So what's your name beside Stickbutt?" Annie asks. She doesn't sit on the sofa next to me, but flops down spraying her soft hair over my face. I smell her perfume— if that is what it is—some sort of odor like scented soap or smelly shampoo. I try to look down her shirt but Milton has already come into the room and he sits down on the arm of the sofa above Annie and he looks down her shirt.

"My name's Roy," I say.

"Roy?" Milton asks.

"My name."

"No you aren't," Milton says. "Your name's Dillon."

"That's not his name." Annie says, "This kid's name is Roy."

"Dillon's my first name. My middle name's Roy, so call me Roy. Roy's a good guy's name."

"You're not a good guy."

"What do you know about being a good guy?" I ask Milton. All Milton knows about is how to break down his motorcycle and how to fix the thing.

"So what're you two doing back here?" I ask. "I was just getting settled and I thought I would sit down and have dinner."

"We scored some hot dogs and stuff from Annie's," Milton says. "How about that?" He jumps off the arm of the couch and he opens the side pocket of the backpack and pulls out hot dogs and buns and mustard and a Heinz ketchup bottle with about half the ketchup pushed to the bottle top. My empty stomach just about buckles from all the excitement.

After we eat the hot dogs, Milton tells me that I have to stay in my room for a while and he and Annie disappear into my parents' bedroom.

I see Milton and Annie leave just as it gets dark. They coast down the driveway with the engine off. They wear army surplus raincoats. The green hoods fade down the street in the darkness and rain.

When I wake up in the morning it's so cold I pull Milton's blankets down from his bunk. I fall asleep again huddled under the heavy pile of blankets. Later Mom comes. She comes down from the woods behind the house and pinches me awake. She says that she was going to get me yesterday but there was a trooper cruiser in the driveway. "Come on Dillon, we're going to meet Dad."

"My name's Roy," I say.

"Come on, Roy," she says.

"What about Milton?"

"Milton's got a bike; he'll turn up on his own."

"When can I have a bike?"

"As soon as you're old enough," she says.

I tell on Milton and tell her that he has a girlfriend named Annie.

"Milton's old enough to take care of himself," she says

as we climb out of the back window and walk up the hill. I look back down to the house where we had lived. I see smoke rising through the rain from some of the other houses down the hill. In the driveway I see the yellow Tonka and I wish like a stupid kid that I can play with it for a moment. "What about your magazines?" I ask Mom. But she's not there. She's already walking into the trees and I hurry to catch her.

A Carpeted Room

———•———

Annie and I owned our own house. I found it abandoned at the bottom of a cul-de-sac where no one had built anything new for years. The roof peak rose from a field of sticker bushes. I had to heave my motorbike through twisting vines that snagged my jacket every few feet. I hid my bike under a moldy plywood panel and then, to hide everything, I cut down some vines with my pocket knife. From the foot of the house we saw only a stand of maple trees. I-5 hissed in the distance like something burning. The lights of the cars fell through the maples around the house like a forest fire.

I stepped on the plywood panel, rocking back and forth until my bike was hid. When I finished, I touched Annie on the shoulder. "Do you like the house?" She just stood still, looking at the ground.

Her shoulders shook as she hugged herself. "Sure, looks fine." She didn't even look at our new house.

I couldn't find Annie's flashlight in all the junk she thought she needed to take with us now that we were going to live on our own. In her backpack, I felt the fuzzy covers of books that had been read too many times, the smooth plastic shells of make-up containers, a roll of toilet paper, and reams of loose wrappers, notebook paper, receipts, garbage. At the bottom of the mess, I came to her flashlight.

We had spent all morning riding along the freeways. I had kept an eye out for state troopers parked in the hideouts along the median waiting to pull over speeders. I figured that Annie's parents would've sent the state troopers after us by now. I could hear her mother's voice on the phone as she dialed the cops, "My daughter's been stolen." She wouldn't say anything like, "My daughter's run away." She'd think I had done it just as I had ripped off her jewelry box and her emergency money. From her viewpoint, I had also taken Annie like a piece of property. In a way I had. We hadn't been going out long enough that we were really, completely, boyfriend and girlfriend.

"Do you smell that?" Annie whispered. I didn't smell anything. While I stood in the doorway of the house, tunneling through Annie's business, I started to see things in the dark living room. Overturned and blackened furniture lay in piles against the walls. The floor buckled and broke where a tree had started to grow through the boards. I flicked on the flashlight and I couldn't see anything for a minute, just the yellow glow around the plastic tip.

"Don't you smell that?" Annie asked again.

"No," I said. "Come on." Annie crowded behind me as I started up the stairs. The steps made a sound like they had just swallowed a bucket of fat. I tried to push Annie ahead of me before the stairs collapsed but she hissed, "I'm not going first." She grabbed me, her hands clutching my neck and her breath pouring into my face. We huddled on the stairs as they groaned under us.

We stepped into an upstairs room carpeted on every flat surface. A thick, orange shag-rug hugged the floor, the walls and the ceiling like the insides of fuzzy dice. Dead Christmas lights hung in arcs from the ceiling and a Lay-Z-Boy—still in its storage plastic—sat in one corner. The old clothes piled on the floor smelled like someone still lived in them.

"Can you smell that?" Annie hissed.

"Yes," I said.

Behind one of the carpets, we found a fireplace large enough for Annie to stand in and look up. "This is it?" she asked me. Her voice echoed against the chimney bricks. Then she ran her hands along the furry walls of the room. I thought we would have to keep looking for a place to stay, but when Annie threw herself on the Lay-Z-Boy and said, "Let's get this rat hole cleaned up," I figured that meant she liked the place.

As we threw the stuff outside, the smell started to go away. I threw the piles of old newspaper and scraps of furniture into the fireplace and we had a bonfire. The flames jumped up into the chimney and the light flickered in the room. Even though we were tired and hungry, we toasted in the fire until we were warm and dry.

My mother had told me about a place where I could work if I ever needed money. She said that the Millionaire's Club in Seattle would let anyone work there. And the good thing, she said, was that after the day's labor they let you keep the money you had earned without skimming off the top and they paid the same day.

My mother was always telling me how to get by in the world without her. We would've just started on one of the spaghetti dinners we always ate, and she would look up and start in on me. "Milton, what did you do in school today?" Read books, I'd tell her. "Milton, when're you going to start to look for a job?" And then she would tell me about job openings she had heard about. I told her that I didn't want to go. After school I would come home, skim through my textbooks, and then run out to work on my motorbike. Mom didn't like my machine. I knew then that one day I would hop on my bike and just clear out. On account of Mom, I knew about all the free meals in the city. I knew how to take care of Annie and me.

Early in the morning, I took the bus downtown before any of the people who worked in the offices showed up. I walked to the Millionaires' Club on Second Avenue and stood behind a crowd of older men. Ahead of me, people stood in clumps, some held Styrofoam cups, others smoked cigarettes. A man right behind me asked, "Do they pay much here? Do they take out income tax? If they do, I don't know if the sweat'll be worth it. No way. I'm just in this to keep me in cigarettes.

"What're you working for?" he asked me.

"Money," I said. I realized when I said this that the word didn't say all that I meant. I meant by money that I could survive next week and Annie and I could sleep with full bellies in a warm room. I realized the man would think I was being a prick.

He grinned. "Money? That's a good one." He put his hands behind his back and looked at me. "You're not old enough to get a job, are you? Like McDonald's, like outside of this kind of thing, are you?"

"I've worked," I said. "I'm eighteen." I lied, but I figured anyone under twenty was young to this guy.

"You can't get legit work, can you?" he said.

"I work," I told him. I started to get pissed at this guy then. Maybe he was mad because I'd been a smart ass. He just stood behind me, knocking something around in his pocket which caused his jeans to bulge back and forth almost as if he had a rat running around in his pants.

"That's not all you can do," the man said. He grinned. He squinted his eyes and pressed his tongue against the back of his teeth. "Not all, is it?"

"No, that's all I've done."

"Yeah? Well, I hope they don't report this kind of money. I just want to keep in cigarettes. You smoke?"

"No. I don't." I didn't smile. I didn't do anything to make him think I thought he was funny or tough.

"Don't drink, don't smoke, what do you do?"

"I drink." I wasn't a kid. I could drink beer just like that. I'd shot-gunned Oly.

"Sure you do, kid," the man said. "Talk to me about it, I can get some booze for you. I'm old enough." He winked and looked down the line of men standing on the side-walk. Their breath clouded around us. "This line doesn't move, does it?"

I turned my back to the man, even though he kept talk-ing. Ahead of me, a truck had stopped and several men hopped in the back. Then a van pulled up and I found myself sitting across from him.

"Hey," he said. "Name's Dwain."

"Yeah?" I said.

"You have a name?"

"Milton." I turned before he could start with me again. I looked into the dark windows of the closed stores. Steam rose from the sewer lids. Then we started on the freeway and finally stopped way out, near the mountains, where Annie and I had come from. My work team spent the day at a dairy farm where we heaved sloppy cattle shit into the back of a dump truck. As I broke through the crusted top, held together by thick green grass, I uncovered cattle shit that smelled far worse than I knew anything could smell. It smelled sort of like the black insides of my motorbike's gas tank. At the end of the day I felt like I had swum laps in a swimming pool of gasoline. When they paid me, though, I didn't care. I held the crisp, clean twenties in the palm of my hand. Forty bucks.

They dumped us off on the sidewalk in front of the Millionaires' Club. I stood looking down the busy street at the cars in the rain and darkness. Dwain raised the palm of his hand to me. "See you," he said.

I said, "Wait, could you do me a favor?"

He stopped and leaned against the wall. "What? Don't you have a place to sleep?"

"I need you to buy me a case," I said.

"A case of what?" For a second I thought he was serious but then he smiled. "Sure," he said.

I walked with him to a convenience store and handed him one of my twenties. I stood outside, smelling the air. My muscles felt like they had turned into old chewing gum. In the store I couldn't see Dwain. In that second I felt like everything inside my head and my stomach and my legs disappeared so that I was just one of those hollow plastic figures you're supposed to fill with candy. I couldn't tell if he was going to come back. I reached for my wallet and I pulled it out. I checked my other twenty and put it back into my pocket. Finally, Dwain came out of the store with the case in a big paper bag. "Here," he said. He dropped some crumpled bills and change in my hand. "You planning on drinking all this alone?"

"No, I've got friends," I said.

He handed me the case. "You sure you don't need a place to stay?"

"No. I've got it covered," I said, "Thanks. Have a beer." I tossed him a can and he caught it with one hand and forced it into his pocket. "See you," he said. But he didn't go anywhere. As I walked away, I turned around and he was still watching my butt.

I came back to the house where Annie and I lived. She had built a fire. I dropped a twenty and ten on top of the recliner. She grabbed them and ran her fingers along the crisp edges. "Watch it," I said. "You'll get a paper cut." She had her hands around my neck and we cozied up on the Lay-Z-Boy. "What's in the bag?"

"Twenty-three cans of Milwaukee's Best," I said.

I watched her as she pulled out two cans. She opened one and tossed me the other. I hadn't had a lot of beer in my life. The few other kids I knew didn't have older brothers, so they had no way of getting beer. When we did drink something—a six pack stolen from a drunken father, the remains of tequila at the bottom of a pint—we had to drink as quickly as possible or we couldn't get a buzz. Annie slammed the first can, draining it straight back, and then opened up another one.

"Drink," she said. I started to drink. I tried to catch her, but she could drink. I closed my eyes and just dumped it into my mouth. I dumped it in and swallowed, opened another can. I lined up cans and did it, just poured it down my throat. We guzzled. We gulped. We drank until our stomachs ached like we had just frozen our guts and the ice block of our guts had pushed out our belly buttons.

"Where. . . how did you learn to do that?" I asked her. Empty and half-empty beer cans lay around the Lay-Z-Boy. "Friends." She brushed the hair back from her face and rubbed beer off her upper lip.

We sat on the chair looking at the fire. I started to think it was too hot when I realized that Annie had put her tongue in my ear. "I love you," she said.

"Love you too," I said. "Where did you first do it?"

"It?" she said.

"Drink beer."

"I don't know. Somewhere."

"That doesn't answer my question."

"No, I guess it doesn't," she said. She stood up on the chair and started taking off her clothes. "Take off your smelly pants," she said. I didn't move until Annie took everything off. She brushed her hands across her ribs. A white fuzz covered her entire body.

As I took off my clothes, I realized how much they smelled like cattle shit. "How come you like me?" I asked.

She pushed me down in front of the fire.

"We don't have to do anything," I said.

"Yeah, right," she said.

We drifted into sleep finally in the quiet room. No one watched Annie and me. No one cared where we were at any time of day or night.

Annie and I agreed that I would work at the Millionaires' Club whenever we needed money. She wanted to get a job. Doing what, I wanted to know? I told her that I didn't bring her out here to make her my slave. We went to the public pool. As we swam around in the hot water, listening to the kids scream as they splashed each other, I knew we had done the right thing, leaving her mom and my mom behind. But also I felt weird. A guy—maybe a year younger than me—was doing back flips because he was showing off for these grade school girls. And I knew a year ago that I could've been him without the muscles. The next day this guy would be going to school. The next day I would be going to work.

A Honda Accord rolled next to the sidewalk as I stood in line the next morning. It stopped by the crowd of old men who had been coming here for decades. "Where's Mike?" a woman said from the car. An old guy looked at me. One of them pulled me by my sleeve and said, "This is a job I think you can handle." He pushed me up to the side of the car.

The window slid down and a woman looked out. Black kinky hair fell down the sides of her head and spilled over her shoulders. Wrinkles spread from the corners of her eyes and deep blue shadows filled the skin around her nose. "Are you looking for work today?" she asked me.

Everyone had left me standing alone on the sidewalk. They stood down toward the Club door with their backs to us, where a U-Haul truck had just stopped.

"I need work."

That song, "Lucky Star," that everyone listened to on the radio, came from her car. Even Annie listened to it. I walked behind the car so the woman wouldn't have to stare at my blue jeans with mud splattered around the cuffs. "Are you hungry?" she asked, as I carefully set my feet on the vinyl foot mat in front of the passenger seat.

"Sure." I ran my fingers along the contoured plastic door grip.

As she drove through the city, stopping at red lights, she didn't say anything. I didn't know what to say to her. I started to say something like, "Nice car," but the words would sound so stupid, I ended up not saying anything. She smoothly parallel parked and, after I slammed the door shut, I found it locked. She walked past a plate glass window that looked into the lobby of a hospital, where a huge man sat in a wheel chair reading a magazine and a security guard trained his eyes on the woman. When I saw the guard looking at her, I looked at her again, seeing what I figured a bored, middle-aged rent-a-cop would see. She had big hips. She had long hair. I figured she must be sort of sexy.

We ate in a mostly empty restaurant. A few other people

sat at small round tables with their faces in the morning *P.I.* The woman set her elbows on the table and looked at me, but I didn't look at her. I paged through the menu. "What can I have?"

"Whatever," she said.

"What're you having?"

"Have whatever you want."

"Thanks," I said.

The waiter stopped at the table. He said, "Hi," in a loud voice. The woman didn't look up. "Dee? How are you? It's been two weeks, two months, years even since you last came in and what do you do, you pretend you're just a walk-in?"

"Hey," she said.

The waiter didn't hold a note pad or anything. He folded his hands across his large stomach, pressing into his belly button, heaving the soft pillow of his white apron around the knot of his fingers. He looked at me. His eyelashes were huge and his skin was pale except for the pink splotches of his cheeks. He raised his eyebrows. "What would you like?" he asked me.

"An omelet," I said. "Apple juice."

"An apple juice omelet?"

"Be nice," Dee said.

"The number twelve."

"Thee numb-bar twelve," I said to the prick.

"Bagel and cream cheese," Dee said. "Coffee extra black."

"Black," the waiter said as he swiveled away on his left foot.

"Have you ever worked for someone before?" Dee asked.

She sat straight against the chair back. Her hair hung down to the middle of her chest. I could tell she had dyed it from the almost blue color that sparkled from the ends. My mother dyed her hair. My brother and I would have to go outside because of the smell. Dee wore a blazer with the cuffs rolled and a white shirt with frills lining the buttons. She smiled. I could tell she didn't mean work like normal work. "No, I think," I said.

"Does that mean no?" she said.

"No," I said.

Dee chuckled, a sound like my motorbike warming up before it begins to hum. Her teeth were large and outlined by a darkness like she had been eating finger paint. The waiter set Dee's coffee cup and my apple juice down. He stood at the table for a moment, looking at me. Dee didn't notice because she was also looking at me. Then the waiter made a *snick* noise in the back of his mouth and rolled into the kitchen.

After breakfast and a drive to her place, Dee said "Sit down, make yourself at home." We stood in her condo, overlooking Lake Union. I sat because I thought she was telling me to. A white sofa with scalloped arm rests lined one wall and turned at the corner. A huge TV entertainment center sat between the two windows facing the water. Everything was new and neat. I was afraid to move. Dee stood in the kitchen opening cupboards and the refrigerator. "What kind of drink would you like?"

"Anything," I said.

"Would you like to watch TV?"

"Sure," I said.

"The remote is on the coffee table."

I held the panel in my hand, I pressed the rubber button for power, and the lights on the TV, the V.C.R., and the stereo flicked on. A clear picture of a man standing in a field in Africa flashed on the screen. I could tell it was Africa because all around him it looked like The

Mutual of Omaha's *Wild Kingdom*. He wore Indiana Jones-type clothes. I could hear the animals snorting in stereo from behind and around me.

"Here," Dee said. She handed me a heavy round glass full of soda water.

We sat on the couch watching the man and then a woman with a weird accent set camp. Servants appeared on the sides of the screen, so I think the man and the woman just sat around and talked while the servants set everything up. I wondered, as I sat there and drank from the sweet soda water, if they drove or if the servants carried everything on their head like in a black-and-white Tarzan movie.

"Finish your drink, you're taking a bath," Dee said.

She watched me as I skinned my blue jeans off. She sat on the toilet and I turned my back to her to pull my socks and underwear off. Water spilled into the tub and steam filled the room. I eased into the hot water without looking at her. When I finally looked up, my skin already turning a bright red, she was sitting on the edge of the tub.

Her bathtub was huge, with chrome handles and spigots that shot hot water. She lifted a plastic bottle of pink bath oil and poured it into the water. She watched the stream of oil as it pooled on the surface and started to mix with the water. The water grew slippery. "Lay back," she said. She took off her shirt and laid it on the toilet and slid her skirt down her legs. She looked like one of the woman in the *Sears* catalogue, except Dee's stomach turned over the edge of her underwear and her breasts bulged around the cups of her bra.

I didn't want to get turned on so I started examining her bathroom. In the organized towel rack, the color co-ordinated bath rug, towels, and soap dish, in all the white walls, I couldn't find anything to make me lose interest. I read an embroidered and framed saying that read:

I wiped away the weeds and foam.
I fetched my sea-born treasures home;
But the poor, unsightly, noisome things.
Had left their beauty on the shore,
with the sun, and the sand, and the wild roar.

There was a naked woman in front of me and I wasn't exactly sure how she had arrived there. As soon as her clothes came off, I lost track of the woman who had taken me to breakfast. Despite the dime-sized mole on the back of her thigh, the dimpled pockmarks in her fat legs, all I could see then was the springy arc of her breasts in the white bra as she leaned into the water, and her black hair as it fell across the white enamel. All I was aware of was the warmth of her breath on my face, and the slight odor of coffee and bacon.

In the water, bubbles spilled and boiled around me but I only felt hot and hotter, though I didn't burn. The naked woman in the clean bathroom put my hand between her legs. The floral smell of the water, the steam, flushed my cheeks. I felt a hard nub in the soft folds between her legs—she kept telling me to touch above it, below it, touch it. Finally it grew rigid. She let out her breath and slipped into the water beside me. She removed her bra and her breasts fell out like Slinkies.

With Annie things were on a beginner level, sort of like the first six or seven times I played *Space Invaders*. It was a comfortable, expected experience, something we did together because we were together and alone in the same room, why the hell not? But with Dee, it was like she had bought a special chair to play *Space Invaders* in. She could blow out the rows of aliens backwards, from the top of the screen to the bottom.

Dee dropped me off in downtown Seattle with fifty dollars I had folded and placed in my sock under the heel of my foot. I didn't want to go home. I didn't want to go home to Annie. Somehow the thought of walking up the steps into the musty and moldy carpeted room made me think of bugs, crawling ones, like worms, millipedes, and grubs. Sometimes doing a landscaping job, I would find a few grubs in the ground. I would push them around with the end of my shovel and think, people can eat these things?

I sat at the docks where all the tourists walked around bumping into each other, not so many as in the summer but still they were everywhere. A man shuffled in front of me and nodded at me. He sat on the bench next to me, grasping the metal handle with his bony fingers. He wore a captain's hat, tattered and torn around the edge. He just sat next to me for a long time. I started to think he wouldn't leave. I don't know why I didn't leave; maybe I thought he would say something important to me. I began to think as we both sat there, him waiting to say something, me waiting for him to say it, that I should tell him what I had done. Finally, he said in a slow voice that sounded like TV snow, "How about a blow for five?"

"Sorry, sir," I said. "I don't need any blow." When I stood up, my knees shook and wobbled like I had just lifted a great weight. I shifted through the people milling around the totem poles, the Indian masks, and the hanging boat oars. I knew what blow was because my father had explained to my brother and me exactly what a pusher called what.

I hurried up to Third Avenue, afraid the junkie would follow me. I didn't stop. When I looked at other people on the sidewalks, I caught them just as they looked away from me.

Flopping into the brown vinyl seat, almost at the back of my bus, my body settled down. I checked out the other passengers, remembering most of their faces from other trips home. One man I assumed worked as a janitor because he always carried a mop, a broom, and a belt covered with various tools. The man leaned against the seat in front of him and stared down into the collection of screwdrivers, pliers, and wrenches, their greasy surfaces scratched to shiny metal. Women in dresses and tennis shoes sat toward the front of the bus. They almost all read books. Their voices didn't carry but filled the bus with a murmur like a tree full of birds. A guy about my age sat in the swivel center section of the bus. He wore a grey stocking cap pulled down to the base of his neck. Another guy, across the aisle from me, caught me looking at him and he stared at me. When I looked to the window to watch his reflection I could see him eyeing me. He coughed and as I turned he said, "What's your problem?"

I didn't say anything. I didn't look at anyone. I just rode the bus. At my stop I jumped off the bus and ran home. I hurried up the creaking steps into the six sides of carpet and the smell of warm wood smoke.

I could tell Annie had been sleeping with someone, someone besides me. I could tell because when I walked through the door she stood and kissed me on the cheek. Her lips felt too soft and too warm, as if she had been kissing someone for hours. She sat drowsily on a wooden chair I had brought up from downstairs. The Lay-Z-Boy held her body heat in the crook of its arms and back. The book she had been reading lay face down on the arm. Everything looked carefully arranged to appear that she had been waiting for me.

"How was your day?" she began, already attempting to divert me from what she had been doing all day. I could tell she had been fucking someone in this room.

"Fine," I said, but I shuffled out of the warm crevice of

33

the recliner, heated by who knows whose body. I circled the room, smelling for other guys. All I could smell was the familiar mustiness of the carpets and the charcoal smoke from the fire.

Annie had me in her arms. "Calm down, what's wrong?" She stroked my neck and I scanned her neck for hickeys, the faithless bitch. "It's all right," she said. "We're doing okay." We rocked back and forth in the middle of the room. The faint odor of the Western Family soap I had bought powdered the triangle at the base of her neck. "Calm, calm, calm," she said.

"What did you do today?" she asked me in a quiet voice like I wouldn't notice.

I threw the money toward the carpet-draped ceiling where the bills fluttered and skimmed to the floor. "I did that," I said. I watched her, waiting for her to make a mistake that would tell me who she screwed that day.

I didn't have to stand in line the next day outside the Millionaires' Club. Dee's car idled across the street. She wore sunglasses and the only thing I could see of her face were her nose, her cheeks, and the wispy line of hair that grew on her upper lip. We pulled into the steep driveway at the base of her building and parked in a garage that smelled like oil and wet cement. She opened a metal door labeled with the word *exit* stenciled in faded spray paint. A stairwell coiled up a cement shaft. The door closed and the sound echoed. I felt her pull me by the shoulders and push me into the dusty space under the last flight. She raised herself above me. I tried to crawl away.

"Stop moving," she said. I lay back in the dust. It coated the back of my head. Her hands gripped my waist. My belt buckle jingled on the pavement and the grooved cement was cold against my butt. It felt like I was being bruised in ruffle potato chip patterns. She still wore her glasses.

"Am I doing okay?" I said. I realized as I said it that I could barely talk. My voice was full of the chalky dust that shifted up and around my head. I rolled, my ear pressed to the ground, and the sound from the vacuum in a bottle filled my head. "Am I doing all right?" I asked.

"Fine," she said. She smiled and licked her lips. A door far up the stairwell opened. It took three minutes, it seemed, for the wide sound of the metal door grating open against the pavement and then dragging shut to end. Dee pushed me further under the stairwell with one hand. She huddled down next to me and wrapped her arms around me. "Quiet," she said, "you're doing fine."

A woman wearing a short skirt and carrying a Nike bag with a racket handle sticking out one end opened the door and I watched her jog across the parking garage as the door slowly swung shut. "She's got a nice ass?" Dee pushed me back to the wall. Dee turned around and told me to get to it.

Finally, in her apartment, in the near darkness—as dark as we could get it because the blinds couldn't close all the way—we watched the rest of the movie I had started watching. But it didn't make any sense as soon as I realized that I had only seen a little of it. "What's this about?" I asked Dee.

"I don't know," she said. She stared at the ceiling with one of her heavy glass tumblers in her hand. She wore her nightgown. "You really should leave," she said.

"Will you let me watch the movie from the start?"

"Not today,"

"Tomorrow?"

"I work," she said. As she stared at the ceiling or somewhere just above her head her glass tipped and ice cubes almost fell out.

"Do you need me again?" I leaned up onto the couch and brushed her arm. She jerked away her glass and spilled ice over her gown. Cubes slipped onto her white couch. Her bathrobe fell open as she jumped. An apron of flesh hung over a curly pile of pubic hair peppered with white. "Fuck," she said as she set the glass down on the table and brushed her hair from her face. I kneeled to pick up the ice cubes. My hands tingled from the handful of ice. My fingers jittered as they slid the cubes back into the tumbler.

Sitting on a stool at the breakfast bar, Dee lit her cigarette and watched me dump the ice into the sink. I turned on the hot water to watch the ice melt. "You should get out. I've got things on my mind."

I didn't say anything. I dried my hands by waving them in the air, wandering through her apartment until I found my clothes at the foot of Dee's bed. My socked feet felt warm in my shoes. I examined the room, the bed sheets heaped on the floor beside her chest of drawers, the wrappers of Alka-Seltzer cold medicine, and the empty bottles of Robitussin heaped on her bedside table, and looked for anything that I had left behind. But I had my Timex and my wallet: anything else was lost and I wasn't about to dig through her stuff to find it.

"Tomorrow?" I asked.

"I told you I work," she said.

"Next day?"

"We'll see."

She opened the door for me. As soon as I stepped into the hallway she closed the door and I knew then that I wouldn't be getting my fifty dollars. Maybe she felt that I was no longer working for her. Maybe she thought I wanted to do all this.

As soon as I came out onto the street below her building, I found myself in a narrow street between office buildings and other apartment buildings. I couldn't even see across the lake through the steady mist. I walked down the sidewalk toward Lake Union. I figured eventually I would come to some sort of street that would take me downtown. At the first intersection I had to wait for a light.

A guy around my age stood at the light with me. He wore a wool cap pulled around his ears. The light turned and we crossed the street. He walked right behind me. I looked up at the office building. We moved under it. It rose above us, four stories of windows. The clouds fell against the plate glass and water trickled down the side and dripped onto the sidewalk. The guy walked so close to me I could hear his boots clomp.

At the end of the office building, he pushed me. His fingers dug into my shoulder, making my sides tingle. He shoved me into the alley. He forced me into a brick court-yard full of green dumpsters. "Hey, Dickboy." I lurched against the wall. He shoved his cap into his coat pocket. Hair spilled down to his shoulders. Except for a thin mustache and a swollen red boil on the side of his face, he looked about my age. Now that I was against the wall, now that he was facing me, everything seemed to slow down. He didn't seem rushed but I felt like someone had jammed a drum kit in my throat.

"What you're doing with my woman? She screw you good?"

"Well—" I started to say.

"Don't answer," he said. "How much you cost?" He grabbed me again. I pulled away from him and socked him in the head or tried to, but he pulled back and kicked me. I fell against the wall and then slid to the ground where he stood on my hand. I felt the asphalt grow extremely hot and then my hand went numb when he took his weight off it. I couldn't get up. When I tried, I jolted back against the wall. I was spastic. I tried to move, but every time I got to my knees he kicked me in the ribs. Finally I just lay on the wet asphalt letting the oily water soak through my coat and my shirt, plastering them to my skin.

"All right," I wailed.

"Go near that woman again and I'll tear your dick off." He leaned down next to me and slapped me in the head. "How much did she pay you? That's my cash." He pulled my wallet out of my pocket and turned it inside out. My social security card fluttered to the ground. "Shit," he said and tossed the wallet next to me.

He turned his back to me. I could have jumped him but I didn't.

On the way to the bus I caught glimpses of myself in windows and I thought I recognized the guy who had jumped me as a sort of version of myself. Maybe a bigger and tougher version of me but he seemed about my age and he looked sort of like me. He needed the money like I needed the money, I figured. The money allowed Annie and me to do anything—it allowed us to live in the house. Without it I would have to get back in the trucks and work in the cattle shit.

I sat in the first seat behind the driver so I could slide down the steps and out of the bus before anyone else could move. I sat there so if I had to move, I could. My clothes smelled from the street water and every time someone sat next to me, they would shift slightly and when the bus stopped they would hurry to other seats further back. As I watched a woman in a trenchcoat carrying a brief case rush away from me, I saw one person who did stare at me. It was the guy in the grey cap. I realized then that I had already seen him a few times before he jumped me. He caught me looking at him and he nodded his head.

I decided I would ride past my stop. I would jump out

of the bus and run faster than he could struggle through the people to the front of the bus and pay. I would run home up the steps and throw something heavy like the Lay-Z-Boy in front of the door.

He never stopped looking at me. Three stops from my stop, the guy started down the bus. He said "Excuse me, excuse me," in a loud voice to the people standing in the aisle. "Hey, shit bird," he said to me, "your stop coming up?" I didn't do anything.

At my stop he rattled his change into the slot and stepped down the steps. "Thank you," he said to the bus driver. He stood on the side of the road and raised his eyebrows at me. I kept on the bus.

When I got to the next stop, I jumped off the bus so quickly I didn't pay. The driver yelled behind me, "Pay!" but I ran. When I looked back, the bus had closed its door and I couldn't see anyone around me. Houses stretched for miles over the top of Beacon Hill and down to Lake Washington where all the black people lived. Mom had always told my brother and me never to come here. I lived here now. Through the thin slices of open living-room drapes the blue TV radiation tainted everything. I could only hear the sound of the trees and the distant airplanes coming down on Boeing field.

I grabbed one of those metal poles that held a street reflector. The thing just lay in the ditch, useless. When I came to my normal stop, I couldn't see the guy. "Come out, you fuck. I'll give you trouble," I yelled.

My yell didn't even cause anyone to part their drapes. I just heard the sound of branches knocking one another, the faint drip of water falling through the bushes, and the last of a descending airplane. I ran down the muddy path toward the house. When I came out of the woods to the house and the distant line of streaking headlights on the freeway, I thought I would see the guy. But I didn't see him anywhere. I stumbled through the front door to the base of the dark steps.

"Who's there?" Annie said above me.

"Me," I told her.

"Who?" Annie said. "Don't move. I have a gun and I'll blow your guts out."

"Me, Milton," I said. I ran up the steps and into our room with its candles and fire and slightly moldy rugs. I closed the door, slid the recliner, and shoved it against the door. "Where's the gun?" I asked.

"Lies," she said as she smiled.

I sat in front of the fire and listened to the sounds outside the room, expecting to hear something but I didn't hear anything.

"I made you a hot dog and chili," Annie said. She pulled the Nalley's can out of the fire and drew the hot dog off its stick. "Sit down, relax," she said. She dumped the chili and the hot dog, coated with spots of charcoal, into a bowl. I could see how young she was. I could see it in her hair that barely grew longer than her shoulders and in her skin. Even the skin under her eyes was clear and I could see her thin blue veins like the ones in my wrist. I ate but my stomach felt like it had shrunk to the size of a bottle cap.

"What did you do today?" she said. She touched me on the side of my mouth.

"What? Why did you do that?" I asked.

"Sorry," she said. She sat next to me, with her arms wrapped around her knees. "Chili was dripping out of your mouth."

Something ticked downstairs in the house like someone had rapped a tin can with a pencil. I didn't want to tell Annie about the guy on the bus, the man who was chasing me. I just ate my chili even though it collected at the top of my shrunken stomach in a big greasy ball. The thought of my bed at home came to me then, sort of like a vision in the fireplace and I wanted to laugh because it looked comfortable. I remembered the stupid little things about waking up after sleeping for a long time in a bed with freshly made sheets, not that it happened in my mother's house very often. I remembered the things I had never thought about while actually sleeping in a bed with sheets that had just been washed. The soapy smell of the sheets and the sizzle of fabric as I shoved my leg around under the covers.

"You are allowed to speak," Annie said. After I had been staring into space. "You tell about your good day and then this is the part where you ask me what I did."

I don't know why I didn't warn her that some crazed madman knew where I lived. I could hear the sound of him on the stairs, the stealthy shifting of his weight on each step so he wouldn't make any noise. Annie didn't notice. I don't know how she could just sit in her place and casually look up at me.

"I went to the library today," she said, "and found you a book about Harleys." She pulled the book out of a brown paper bag. It was huge, bigger than any book I had actually held in my hands. I laid it in my lap. Almost every page had a full color photo of a motorcycle with bikers straddling them or slutty women thrusting their chests up. Annie sat next to me brushing my hair back with one hand. "Do you like it?"

"Sure," I said.

"You don't like it," she said.

"Yes," I said. "I like it. What else did you do today?" I said then. I heard the guy in the grey cap jiggle the door handle. "Quiet," I said.

"You are such a liar," she said. "You hate the book. You hate it." She jumped up on the recliner. "Why do you keep me here if you hate me?"

"Be quiet," I told her but she started yelling and yelling.

"I can say anything I want," she yelled.

Annie didn't understand anything about our situation and I don't think she wanted to. She wouldn't want to go back home to her mom. I couldn't stay here. I grabbed her and cupped her mouth. She tried to bite me, but I just pressed her head against my chest and held her. "Quiet, quiet," I said. We listened but didn't hear anything. At any moment the door might swing open and there he would be.

The Lake On Mars

———•———

Art insisted that our troubles came from the government's persecution of us. "We won't follow the rules," he said. "We live by our wits and they won't take that kind of crap from anyone." I figured they harassed us because we had been selling as much pot as we could grow to a man the Feds had busted on Christmas Eve. Art saw it differently. He said that we were fugitives because we were Individualists, as if that were a dissident political party like some 1920's communists. Instead of Bolshevik beards our friends wore a uniform of black Hanes T-shirts and ragged blue jeans.

Any way we looked at it, the county pigs had found us at Paul Lane's house and told us we had better get moving because they were tired of our type in their neck of the woods. We started to pull everything together and prepared to get on our way. We rented a cheap room. I worked overtime and Art tried to cover as many shifts at the Chevron as possible. As soon as we had enough money, we left.

I always thought I'd do anything to stay with Art. He wore a pair of wire-rimmed glasses and a short manicured beard. When he wore his old turtleneck sweater I would go crazy and start cradling my chin in the crook of his neck and running my hands over his strong back. Together, we started out on this crap and I figured I'd stick it out for as long as it lasted. I believed I wasn't about to find anyone better. Art can be real sweet in a pinch. I liked to think of Art as a poet stuck behind the wheel of a Chevy Supersport Impala.

The car had plenty of room for our oldest son, Milton, who had just returned from God knows where, to curl up against the black leatherette in the Pony Express blanket that he had slept in every night since he was five years old. For ten years, every night, Milton demanded that I give him this blanket to sleep in. Even when it was ice cold in the boys' bedroom, he only slept with this blanket. Under it, he wore his coat and jeans, looking like some bum who had momentarily settled in for the night. The only time, that I knew of, that Milton had ever left his blanket behind was when he took off three months ago.

Art and I didn't know how long Milton had been gone at first, because we were in Monroe storing all our stuff in our friend Paul Lane's basement. We were momentarily delayed by some coke Paul had picked up and a new stereo system; all his records sounded startling on that stuff. When we returned home, Dillon, my youngest son, was still in the house but Milton had taken off. "Don't worry," Art had said. "He's at an age where he needs to establish his own identity." But I was worried. "Quit mothering him," Art had said.

In my *Redbook*, I read an article about people's pets, about the stuff animals do when people aren't around. The article profiled a cat who visited the neighbor's cat and the two would go on trips together. They would wander to a nearby river and roll down the bank and sleep under a tree and go home, sort of like a mini-*Incredible Journey*. I started to think how this applied to kids. I thought about the things kids did when adults weren't around. I wondered how Dillon and Milton behaved that week Art and I hung out in Monroe. In a way, I figured, it was like the moment when you finally went to Open House at the elementary school and discovered that your kid had a whole other life that you knew nothing about. Your kid had friends who stood directly behind their parents so that you had to shake this adult stranger's hands and say, "My son has said so much about your son, I feel like I know you."

Milton came back different. His head brushed above mine now. With his darker peach fuzz he looked older until you noticed just how smooth his skin was. He didn't say much when he came to the door of our room at the Mount Si Inn. Paul Lane had told him where we were, which was a good thing, as we had already started to pack that night and in the morning we would have been gone.

When Milton came through our motel room, I remembered his way of walking. He walked like he was ducking under a low door frame; with each step, he lowered his head. He crouched across the room and sat at the kitchen table. He didn't say any of the usual things he would say to Dillon. He just sat at the table and asked if he could make himself some coffee. "Sure," I said, looking up from my magazine. The only thing I asked Milton was if he had found a job. But he cleared his throat and told me he really hadn't found anything and that was why he was back.

I figured it was a good thing that I had packed the blanket because Milton took it in his hands as soon as I handed it to him and he curled up on the floor between the twin beds and went to sleep.

He hadn't uncurled from the back seat yet, even though we were well on the way in the Impala. He just sat in the back of the car and stared out the window. Sometimes he read from his *Conan* book. Dillon asked Milton if he would play Hangman but Milton just rolled his eyes and went back to reading.

We were on the way to grandmother's house, except we didn't sing any songs and we hadn't seen Mom since she started to visit the hospital in Wenatchee once a week for chemotherapy. She didn't look so good in the picture she had sent for Christmas and that was six months ago. I think she chose to send the worst picture she could find. She stood against the twisted dwarf cherry tree in her back yard. White snow heaped on the branches. Scabs of ice clung to the black bark. Everything looked like hell.

Dillon kept up a constant stream of syllables as he counted mile markers and then because they were not going by fast enough he started counting oncoming cars. Milton started socking Dillon in the arm whenever a truck passed. I should've stopped him but it sort of broke Dillon's stride, so I let Milton get away with it until Dillon screamed. I said, "You two should stop it." But it was a little too late and I was a little too intimidated by Milton's sudden oldness to make him stop. He kept it up and Dillon began to cry. "Make him stop," Dillon said through a wet throat.

"Milton," I said. "We will pull over and Art will knock some sense into you."

"Yeah?" he asked. He didn't say anything after that until we came to Snoqualmie Pass and then Milton said, "What're you going to do to put sense into me? You pair of old potheads." He socked Dillon in the arm so hard that something snapped in his younger brother's shoulder. Dillon lost it. He started beating the side of the car and hollering. Art snorted and pulled the car to the wide freeway shoulder. Gravel popped under the tires and the sun slipped under the trees. The car stopped and the traffic behind us laid on their horns as they zipped around us.

Art chewed on his lower lip and took off his glasses. He flapped his arm over his bucket seat. "Okay punk, my father said this to me when I was fifteen: 'If you live with us, and if it comes to a fight, you better knock me on my ass because if you don't, if you provoke me, I'll break your jaw.' Understand?"

Milton and Dillon, Art and I, didn't say a lot after that.

When our cherry 1967 Supersport Impala, its chrome bumpers cleaned by some electronic process at a detailing shop where Art had spent thousands, shot over Snoqualmie Pass, the smell of prairie and pine trees dusted us. The smell was Mom. She constantly washed everything she owned, watered her lawn, or applied moisturizer to her skin from pink jugs she bought from the Sprouse Ritz in Ephrata. When Mom wanted to say something was old or worn out she said it was dry, as if the word dry carried some extra meaning for her; dry skin looked like worn-out Naugahyde or ancient skin bunched around old eyes. When I first heard someone described as having a dry sense of humor, I thought they meant that they had an old-fashioned sense of humor. By applying water, Mom tried to restore everything, to make the grass in her yard as green as green could be, to make her skin smooth and young.

Six years ago Mom still had what remained of her former bombshell self. I imagine that most men would have still slept with her. I always thought Mom should have been a movie star. And from the way she talked about her past, I think she believed she was on her way to becoming something great when she met my father.

"Milton," Art said in a low voice, "stop kicking the back of my seat. Sit up straight." As I turned to look into the back seat, Art said, "Stop shifting, you're throwing the car off balance."

"Please," I said, "I could stand up and belly dance and not throw this car off balance."

When I turned to look at Milton, he said in a loud voice, "I'm not doing anything now."

"I was just looking at you," I said.

"Stop," he said. His face turned colors as he looked at me; red splotches spread out from his ears. I smiled a stupid smile the way I do when a dog leaps out of a driveway barking, teeth clicking, but Milton still stared at me.

I took a quick peek at Dillon, but he was drawing what looked like mountains—huge triangles with spiky growths spraying out of the sides—in a notebook I had been using to keep track of bills. "Nice notebook," I said. Dillon didn't stop scratching lines into the paper.

"We need to pull over," Dillon said.

"We'll be in Moses Lake in forty minutes," Art said. "Hold your hose."

I turned on the radio and plowed through the static until I came to Debbie Harry singing *Rapture*. As the song ended, Art laughed. "Let's get some pure proletarian music pumping." He fished under his seat and pulled out his plastic tape case, half filled with tapes, the other half filled with Zig Zags and baggies of his ragweed. He snapped in *Exile on Main Street*. The tape was so worn that anyone who was normal couldn't identify it because every letter had been rubbed off.

Dillon started to tap me on the shoulder. "I need to go," he said.

"Could you pull over?" I asked Art. He smiled at me, his hair flapping around his glasses. He put one hand on the arc of my neck.

"I love you, but we aren't stopping." He said this like it was some sort of big deal. "We get to your Mom's house. We say Hi. We say Bye, and then we are on our way. He can go there."

Dillon rocked back and forth against the back of the seat.

"You are such a pussy," Milton said.

"We should pull over," I said to Art. He didn't say anything. "Can you hold it, honey?"

"No."

"Art, just pull over," I said.

Art slammed on the breaks. We all jerked forward. Dillon leaned out of the driver's-side door like someone had just knifed him in the side. He staggered behind the car, and leaned on the trunk. A station wagon with a metal boat on the roof slid over the horizon and sped by. Dillon sat in the ditch.

"What's taking you so long?" Art asked.

"There are cars going by," Dillon said.

While Dillon turned into the ditch, Art let go of the brake and the car lurched forward and rolled down the road. Milton laughed, not like he thought anything was funny but like someone who had just discovered a pickle in his underwear. An eighteen-wheeler lifted over the horizon with a line of cars behind it. They whistled past us and a few cars honked their horns at Dillon who was zipping up his pants and running after us.

After the stop, Art started to speed. He jammed on the gas and the Impala crept up to a green hatchback. He swung our car across the double yellow and sped past the car. He raced up to the next car and started hugging its bumper.

He shot the Impala over the yellow divider to pass a Trans-Am that must have been going 65 miles an hour. An oncoming windshield a few hundred yards ahead of us glittered just over the watery waves of heat and Art stepped on the gas. The engine roared and the mass of the car lurched forward. I wasn't in any hurry to reach Mom's house but I was in plenty of a hurry to get Art off the road. I've always felt awkward needing things from sick people, but I needed to see Mom before Art and I began our trip to who knows where because I didn't know when we would be back this way again. The car coming toward us sounded its horn, a brassy noise that made the tips of my fingernails ache from digging into the leatherette seat. Art crossed back over the yellow and the Trans-Am behind us blew its horn.

"We are on our way," Art said.

He turned up the volume on the Stones. I suppose that the ancient echo of Mick Jagger's voice and Keith Richards' guitar would have given me flashbacks if there had been a gap between then and now. Art seemed to think history started somewhere in May 1967 and faded to a stop on side two of Pink Floyd's *Dark Side of the Moon* sometime in 1973. Art used this music not to pass the time, but to tread water in the present. Unlike him, I needed new songs.

He lurched the car around a camper and almost ran through an oncoming Honda motorcycle. "This should be a three-lane road," Art said as he jockeyed in front of the camper.

"What? Is there oncoming traffic?" I said. "I hadn't noticed."

Art smiled at me, wrinkling his forehead the way he

has always wrinkled his forehead. There was a time when I actually thought the faces he made were cute.

When Art and I watched the moon landing we had popcorn and beer and put the light out as if the landing were a football game. He kept slipping his arm around me and making a surprised noise when I didn't throw his hand off my breast. It was an okay time because we were in our black-and-white world watching Neil Armstrong go out into space. Under the blanket on the couch I cupped Arthur between the legs and rubbed him while we watched the TV. Milton lay in his crib. He didn't cry. Arthur and I were back in the world we had been in before Milton, before we started dating, when I had already watched enough men gingerly taking off their underwear to fill a football field and my husband had stood at the foot of enough beds gingerly taking off his boxers to fill a Holiday Inn. While we lay in our apartment watching the man standing on the moon we felt for some reason that we could have been in Art's parents' apartment. We needed the blanket to cover up my touching him as though the people on TV would suddenly focus on us.

Finally we came to a long line of campers, trucks with aluminum fishing boats strapped on top, and station wagons. Art gunned the car into the oncoming lane, into the yellow line winding around the edge of the hill and into the prairie.

Art pulled into Mom's short driveway. Her yard grew in green bristling blades where the other yards twisted into tight patches and clumps of yellow grass. Mom stood on the porch squinting at us and watering her yard from a long, green garden hose. She wore a new wig, bright and red, like a colorized version of Lucille Ball. I checked Art, and he stared at her as though he had just discovered that Mom was a zebra and I was a zebra and he'd been putting his dick in a zebra all these years.

Dillon scrambled out of the back seat and rushed past Mom. She stood on the cement pad at the foot of her kitchen door, her hands on her hips, the globe of her red hair hanging in the air like a permanent fire work. Dillon ducked under her and barked, "Hey, Grandma." Milton walked after Dillon. As Mom tried to touch him he stood back. He shifted around her as though he had bumped into a wall. She looked at me as Milton did this. What was I supposed to do? I shrugged. They were my kids. I didn't have any control.

"I thought you'd be later than this," Mom finally said. She wore a light green party dress, short enough that it showed off her legs which were still much better than mine. Years of waitressing had exploded my veins so that my thighs looked like tubular maps of the canals of Mars. The light green dress complemented Mom. She looked like a pastel Christmas tree. But I didn't say anything.

As soon as we entered the kitchen, Mom said, "Please excuse the mess." We sat at her kitchen table. Gene Vincent sang from a small black radio. A pink fuzzy creature made of two felt balls hung from the antenna. We took our places at the table, each of us, I think, planning how we would say what we had to say, and planning how we would fake out everyone else so they couldn't say what they were going to say. Then Mom said, "I'm dying, you know." She lit a cigarette and held it up to her lips, holding Art's and my attention in the moment when we didn't know what to say. Mom had painted her lips a red that somehow didn't clash with her hair, but under the paint I could see the thick wrinkles of her lips. She had used her lips like a plumber used his hands; her lips had scooped all the shit that they could move for fifty-odd years and now she was sitting at the table and I don't think she cared about much anymore, least of all telling us crap.

On the edge of the kitchen table, stacks of newspaper starting with the crisp black and white of this morning's *Tribune* fell into yellow pulp. She must not have read her paper for six months.

I didn't know what to say to her. On the one hand it was true, I think, that she was dying. But when she just said it, it made it seem like a lie. My father did not complain before his death. My father, when he was alive, filled the house with his smell, a sweet, alcoholic odor like cologne and he would sit in the only wooden chair that would hold together and watch Ed Sullivan and then turn in, leaving his smell to linger through the house like we had momentarily moved to the perfume counter at Woolworth's. After my father died, nobody I knew watched Ed Sullivan. When we visited his plot at the cemetery, we could only smell grass and the pungent reek of milkweed growing in the reservoir. I know, though now it's difficult to recall, that Mom once had brown hair that waved in tight swells down her back and curled into her waist. When she stood under the lamp doing dinner dishes, her like electric filaments. Now she was bald and no matter what we'd done, what Art had done with her, we had to spend time with her. But I wondered how I would think of her after she was gone and I could barely remember her as she had been.

"I'm leaving Art," I said.

Art took off his glasses and lay them on the table. "How am I supposed to respond to this two-pronged attack?"

"Say you're sorry," Mom said.

"I'm sorry. Really, I'm sorry that you're sick," he said to Mom, and then glanced at me. "I'm sorry that you've gone off the deep end. You two feel better now?"

"I'm serious," I said. "I'm not hysterical. We're done with you."

"Who's we?" he asked.

"Me and the kids."

"I'm dying here," Mom said.

Art laughed. "Excuse me," he said.

"Okay, Mom, tell us. Tell us how you're dying."

"You've always been like this, you know? You have to be the one in charge. Listen to you telling me when I can speak. You never could let yourself just go along for the ride."

"Who's riding who?" I asked.

"How can you say that to a woman who's about to die?"

"Please tell us," I said. "Go ahead, Mom, and tell us."

Art and I listened to her talk about going to the hospital. She didn't know any of the doctors there, even though she had been going there for almost a year. They told her when she had the results back from her first test that she couldn't count on six months. "They were trying to kill me. It would save my insurance company money—that's what I think." She coughed and smoke sprayed from her lips. "I don't count on anything anymore. A month, a year, it's relative. What is two of this for one of that?" She smiled.

"I'm sorry," I said.

"Keep it for yourself, honey," Mom said. She fingered one of the long strands of her wig. It was a gigantic head of hair. If I only glanced at it, it looked sort of real even with the explosion of unnatural color and length. It was as if the radiation had resulted in an abnormal tensile strength of hair, like the way our lawn used to grow in absurdly healthy patches after the service truck spilled oil by the tank.

I stood out of my chair, aware suddenly that Mom and Art were both looking at me. I wanted them to say something but they had stopped. "I need some water," I said.

"Eight glasses a day," Mom said, "drink at least that much. It's a lot of water, I know. We have juice, coffee, tea, club soda. Would Milton and Dillon like some soda?"

"I don't know," Art said. He picked up the morning paper.

"Would you like some coffee?" I asked Art.

"Not this instant." He rattled his paper as if to show me he was otherwise occupied. I opened a cupboard, removed a tin of coffee grounds and snapped the lid off.

Mom, at the entry to the living room, said, "Dolls? Would you like some soda?"

"Sure," the dolls said.

"Are you actually giving them club soda?" asked Art as Mom opened the refrigerator door. The broken seal snapped in the warm room. I turned the coffee machine on and the percolator bubbled.

"What's wrong? Aren't they allowed soda?"

"Eloise, kids don't like club soda."

"They wanted some."

"You asked them."

Mom opened the freezer; thick ice floes hung on the aluminum and icicles draped to the top shelf. "They would like some, they said they would," she said. I watched her walk into the living room, planting each step and then carefully taking the next one. Her hips almost swayed too far, sending her to the ground. Then her other foot planted and she swayed too far the other way.

The coffee machine hissed, steam rose from the plastic roof, and the smell of beans, metallic and earthy, lifted from the machine.

Mom sat back at the table and flicked a battered tin case open, tapped a cigarette on the lid, making a dull rattle, and snapped a match.

I smiled.

"They took it," she said.

"Club soda is only good with gin," Art said.

I heard a thump in the living room and saw Dillon lying on the floor. Milton kicked Dillon in the side of his chest. He stooped over Dillon and leaned into the kick. "Stop, you stupid animal!" I said. I pulled Milton back. He threw my arms off and flashed around. I stared into his eyes and in that second I saw the new person he had become, the new peach-fuzz-turned-mustache and the shaggy spikes of uncut hair. "You two come with me," I said. "Let's go swimming, let's go out and calm down from the trip."

In the kitchen, Art and Eloise stopped talking when I reached down to pick up my keys. Art looked at me and smiled. "Can I have some coffee?" he asked.

"Get it yourself, the kids and I are going swimming with Mom. Come on, Mom."

"I just drove for two and a half hours to this?" Art asked.

"Stay here."

"No. I'll come along."

"We'll be back," I said. "We aren't leaving yet."

"I can stay and keep Art company," Mom said.

"Come on, Mom," I said.

Art looked at me. He dropped a baggie filled with green bud and some papers on the kitchen table. "Have fun," he said.

In *Foundation*, by Isaac Asimov, a group of future scientists use numbers so well that they can predict the future by careful analysis of the past. They are almost right but they forget to take into account the rise of individuals who can change history and thus the future, like Elvis Presley.

Mom always believed that she had fallen from a great destiny. She thought she had made some mistake a long time ago, slept with my father, for instance, and gone down the wrong track. For a long time she said it was because she married Dad, and then she said it was because she allowed herself to drink vodka, and then it was because she had cancer. Each disaster in her life convinced her that if it hadn't happened, something great would have happened.

I drove Art's lumbering Supersport down a gravel road toward Soap Lake's beach. The arid hills around the lake, with sage brush balled into black shadows, like the rock-strewn plains of Mars. The late afternoon sun reflected from the surface made it the metal sheet of a polished grill. A few seagulls—stark white against the reddish gravel—hobbled forward as we closed the car's doors.

"The beach looks like poison," Dillon said.

"Looks like Hell," Milton said.

My mother leaned against the car, looking oddly beautiful in the light that fell across the lake and the wind that flapped the hem of her dress up. She looked like a star of a 1950's B movie, a bombshell right out of the *Forbidden Planet*. She smiled at me and adjusted the explosion of her hair.

A levee built of pock-marked Eastern Washington rock broke the waves far into the lake. A lifeguard tower, its metal corroded into boils and scabs, held a sign that read, "Beach closed until July 1st. No life guard on duty." It was the twentieth of June, but my kids didn't notice the closed sign. They stood on the shore with the waves pouring around their toes, their feet sinking slowly into the murky region where the beach dissolved into the water. The beach showers, four thin pipes, rose on a long wooden frame, the heads twisted toward the ground like the antenna of spacecraft in *War of the Worlds.*

"I won't spray myself under those," Dillon said, sounding almost as though he was speaking right into my ear.

Mom and I sat on a cement bench while we watched the kids play in the lake. Milton blew up a green raft while Dillon waded into the shallows. He splashed water into the air and it sprayed over the rolling silver swells leaving black rings. "Don't go too far," I yelled. The words sounded like the million yells Mom had yelled at me—the million yells I had never listened to.

"They'll go too far," Mom said.

"Yeah," I said, "how far is that?"

Mom smiled at me. "Out beyond the last buoy would be too far." She took off her wig and laid it in her lap like an overstuffed animal. Her head looked small with wisps of hair plastered to her scalp.

"Mom, you can get better. Cancer is not necessarily a death sentence."

"Sweetheart," Mom said in the voice of a movie seductress, "life is a death sentence."

"You're just a little guide book to life today, aren't you?"

"This is it," Mom said. "I've got it all done. A moment like this with you and my grandchildren on a nice day at the beach, that is news. This is an event."

"Good, Mom, just put your hair back on."

I took my shoes off and walked down to the beach into the cool waves. I squatted down to the surface and scooped up a handful of water. In that cup of dark blue water I saw hundreds of almost microscopic, red brine shrimp twirling around, bumping into each other. I dropped the water back into the lake and my skin felt filmy, like it was coated with soap. In the millions of gallons filling the basin I felt the crowds of shrimp, the trillions of them.

"I'm glad you came," Mom said. She stood next to me. Her hair was back on her head.

"We aren't staying the night," I told her. "We'll not stay the night, that is, the kids and I won't stay. I'm leaving Art with you."

"Thank God for small favors," Mom said. She looked out to where the boys were swimming. Standing there, I saw that my mother's wig was completely fake. I could see both the face she had with the wig and the one without it, and the two separate impressions were Mom's face, now. Like a moment of deja vu, I could remember what Mom's face had looked like six years ago when Art and I had come to visit her. It had been fuller then and the skin was smooth and glowed with her manic health. I remembered her holding me years before and telling me that it was all right and I was in her arms and they felt like the entire world. I took my mother in my arms now. She was a bag of lawn clippings, springy and thin. I heard her sobbing then. "Mom, I understand what happened," I said, although I didn't.

"You don't have to go," she said. But I couldn't say anything back.

I looked out into Soap Lake and I thought I saw Milton pushing Dillon under the water. I saw him doing it. I saw him because Milton's shoulders rose above the surface of the lake and I could see him rising up on Dillon's back and Dillon's arms thrash in the water, his face turned down into the brine shrimp where I imagined him looking through the blue depths at the shrimp swimming down and down into darkness.

I didn't move for a second. Then I was running out to the levee and along the gravel road at the top, yelling, "Stop it, stop it!" I felt my toe nails straining against the impact of the stones in the levee. My breath hissed in and out and I felt like I could barely move. I still ran. I ran until I found myself in Soap Lake and I was pushing myself over the choppy waves.

Finally I had Dillon on the shore. I pushed down on his stomach and squeezed his cool skin until I felt his skeleton in my hands; I was afraid I would have to break his bones to wring the water out of him. When I finished, when Dillon coughed and coughed, I looked at Milton. Milton stood behind me, not looking at us, but staring out into the light above the water.

"Is he all right?" Milton asked. And I could see then, or I hoped that I could see it, that Milton wanted Dillon to be all right. I wondered what he was thinking when he pushed his thrashing brother's head under the water toward the darkness. I wondered how an action like this could happen and I didn't know. I didn't know how I had pulled Dillon out of the water and made him breathe again. I didn't know how Dillon had come from me. I had felt the process of him growing inside me, and then I felt the absence of him inside me and he was breathing in the world in front of me as alien as anything I could imagine.

"Is everything okay?" Mom asked. "Can't he swim?"

"He's not a strong swimmer," I said. I helped Dillon to his feet. He hacked up water and the four of us stood on the beach as the light faded. We would sleep in a motel later and I would call Arthur sometime, but I wanted then to remake my kids, rename them, take away whatever had happened to them, take over their private lives, let them start again, step back and let them be whole.

Rehabilitation

———•———

Art Graham
King County Jail
Seattle, Washington
January 20ᵗʰ, 1984

Dear Janice,

I, Arthur W. Graham, am not guilty of any crime, even though I have been convicted of one. I do not say that I am innocent or that I did not do what they said I did, which was sell a policeman 84 ounces of marijuana in a brown grocery bag from Safeway, each ounce wrapped in an individual plastic baggie, just as you yourself have done a hundred times before. This crime, this stupid law that I have broken, does not make me evil. I'm as much of a criminal as a kid breaking a school rule. Selling weed isn't a crime.

You told me that you couldn't be married to a criminal. I have a number of things to say to that. One, as I have already pointed out, I'm not a criminal.

Two, you are my wife. We are married. We made prom-

61

ises to each other; how could you just back out on them and the kids like that? You married me, that means you love me. How could you back out on the man that you love?

Three, I stuck by you. So what if I'm a criminal now? I stayed married to you even though you were fat.

Four, you helped me do it. So what if I was the one they caught? You watered the plants. You smoked the bud. You helped me. You still have our pipe. Do you smoke it with your new friend? I bet the two of you have smoked all our stuff and here I sleep every night in a cold cell with a real criminal, some guy who won't even tell the rest of us what he did.

He talks in his sleep and I listen to him and listen and listen because I think I heard him say one night something about burying a body off on the side of Tiger Mountain.

I'm not sure if you will write back but I wanted to clear my name.

Your Loving Husband
Art

Frederick W. Graham
Veterans Hospital
New Haven, Connecticut
13 Feb 1984

Janice & Artie,
Well, well:
I sure was pleased to hear from you. I sure hope to hear from your mother one of these days. I miss all of

you terrible, Art, and you better believe it too. Janice, you are the very best thing that ever has happened to Art. Art has not had it easy but now I hope he can. I don't mean work wise, I mean home life. Art how big a lawn do you have? Now, guess what I want for Christmas. Well now look, I want a picture of you and Janice. You know about six by nine, I guess, regular size. No frame as I want to make my own. I have a lot of things stacked away and one day I'm going to build a nice cabin and gather up all my things. This is no dream as I already have shopped around for a good single lot and I guess it will be around Deer Park, north of Spokane.

Now, about my condition. Well Art, I'm much better and honest to God, no cancer. You see, I was right in cutting out of that Spokane Hospital. I just had a hunch I didn't have cancer even after he had set up the operation date; so I cut out. Now these new doctors just started from scratch. First x-ray showed growths all through my system. The Doctor says, so we'll take one out and send it to a pathologist and in the meantime you are to be fed IV, as they call intravenous feeding. "Man you are just bones," he said. I weighed 128 pounds and Gene had to help me into the hospital. I couldn't eat nothing. Well imagine my surprise when in came the doctor one evening saying, "Man, this won't keep until morning; no cancer, but your red blood corpuscles are eating up your white ones and in ten minutes you are starting on whole blood transfusions and the swellings are enlarged lymph glands and we can bring them to normal by radium isotopes and you're going to be just like a new man before long now!" That doctor shook his head and said, "Be prepared for some rough treatment for a while." Well rough she was but I'm coming up hill now and I'm making my own white corpuscles, also the glands are way down and I'm getting stronger every day.

Uncle Forrest and Uncle Gene was up to see me yesterday. Forrest looks like a million bucks. Draws 100 per cent pension and 100 per cent social security. He drives a new car, dresses like a Wall Street banker, and doesn't booze very much. He has sure changed. He can work long enough to make $1650 per year and comes here to do so in the winter. Gene's business is very good and getting better all the time, as it should as he does great work and has a good business head and everyone likes him, as they do Forrest. It's good to see someone make good.

I can throw a rock into Long Island Sound from here. Right by New London sub base. I still can hardly wait to get back to good old Washington State. Have not had a drink since I been here. Forrest sure treats me good, no questions asked. I miss your mother sometimes almost more than I can stand but I have to stand it until I get better, no choice. I know when I'm holding a losing hand every time. I never gave Grant County as good a looking over as I wanted to, as I was sick and getting low on loot. I stayed around a week in Snoqualmie because someone swore to me they seen Laura there, but she might have just been passing through. I should have tried Coulee City longer but, as I say, Money! Money! Well some day they can find me, right now I got a fight on my hands and I aim to win. Cold here today. Now my good people, write me and be as good as you can and good to one another above all. Be happy too, as life is queer. I sign off now with much love to both of you forever.

Old Dad

King County Jail
Seattle, Washington
February 17th, 1984

Dear Jan,

Jim Coil, my cell mate, told me what he's doing here. He's just waiting to be taken down to Oregon to be tried for a double murder. He broke into his girlfriend's house and kept finding her with different men.

The first time he broke in, he crashed through her plate glass window. The man ran out of the bedroom in a pair of boxers, swinging one of those gigantic wooden forks that people hang on their walls. It must have belonged to Jim's girlfriend. Jim ducked under this guy and started to choke him. Pam came in with the spoon that matched the fork and smacked the guy she had just been with on the head. She hugged Jim and told him she wouldn't do it again.

A few days later Jim lost his job and came home in the middle of the day. He tried the door. The door was locked. As he set his bag of groceries in the kitchen he heard the noise of his girlfriend going at it in the bedroom. He snuck in there and caught her with a different guy. What was Jim supposed to do?

He and Pam went out for dinner that night at Black Angus. While they ate their steaks he told her he would have to kill her if she slept with anyone other than him.

Two months later, Pam told Jim she was moving out. Where to, Jim wanted to know. I'm moving to Oregon, she said. Who with? No one you know, she said. He had tried to make her a wife and she just didn't work out. So Jim followed her and her new boyfriend to Oregon where she was moving into his apartment. Jim soaked both of them in kerosene and burned them and their building to the ground.

The guards tell me that there's nothing to do for a guy like Jim. He's going to go to prison and stay there. You can't fix a guy like that, one guard told me. "The wiring's off in his brain. When you've got a toaster that always burns your bread," this guard said, "you throw it out."

I don't know. I'm not a toaster. Don't throw me away. We can work things out.

Your Loving Husband
Arthur Graham

King County Jail
Seattle, Washington
February 21st, 1984

Dear Jan,

I have something to tell you, something I never told you when you asked me to tell you something that I hadn't told you before. Since you are not returning my letters or answering the phone, I will tell you.

My mother used to cut my hair in the late fifties before I started going to the barber. We were really poor because she had just left my father. I'd sit shirtless in the kitchen. The water that she used rolled down my back. The silver flash of the scissors, their blades sliding over each other, made every hair follicle on the back of my neck clench so tight that my hair stood up. After my mother finished, it looked like someone had pressed half of a very hairy coconut to my head.

My mother didn't use a mirror. She gauged the evenness of the bowl line by looking at me. After my hair was cut I swept the brown strands into a pile. I dropped it into a brown bag from the grocery store.

When I was old enough, my mother took me to the barber in Snoqualmie. On the way to his shop, she told me how in the very old days people used to go to the barber to get bled. My mother said that people, then, thought that blood carried sickness in it. So they would drain out the sick blood. By the time we got to the barber I thought it would be like a meat shop or something, with odd tools hanging from hooks and fluorescent lights and a man in a special bleeding suit.

Instead, the shop was small and poorly lit except for a row of lights around the mirror. It was so dark, I could hardly see into the back of the room. He only had one chair.

He was small and gray, but his hair was dyed a black so black it looked the hair of King Kong. I sat in the unfamiliar vinyl-backed chair—it even had a special platform for me to rest my feet on. He put a white apron over me, fastening it at my neck. In the mirrors—the walls were covered with mirrors—I could see myself. I saw the chairs back into forever. My bowl head was reproduced forever. He snipped carefully until my hair no longer looked like the Cannibal King's head. I had hoped for a head shaved like everyone else in school. He parted the hair in the middle as if I were a 1930's vegetable seller in an Al Capone movie. He swept the hair into two wings. When he turned the buzzer on, I shrunk into the blanket. Don't worry, he said, and he tossed a bloody ear into my lap.

I screamed. I threw the floppy body part onto the floor where it bounced.

My mother leaned over and picked it up. It's fake, she said.

The barber cut my hair and when it was done I walked down the sidewalk in Snoqualmie catching myself in the windows of the stores. I still didn't look like anyone else I knew.

Love You, Art

———•———

Art Graham
King County Jail
Seattle, WA
February 29th, 1984

Dear Jan,

I'm going to be released tomorrow and then I'm going to be on probation for two years. I would like to get together with you. I've been thinking and as soon as I find you, for sure, everything will be all right. Maybe we can go to the party Paul Lane is going to throw for me when I'm out of the clink? We can go on a date or something?

A couple of the guards from the jail said they'd like to drop by. One of them has been slipping me joints since he found out what I was in here for. He wants me to fix up him with someone who can get him some sweet bud.

I just want to be honest with you, like I have always been, well, pretty much honest. But you know that as soon as everything is back to normal, I'm just going to go back to doing what I have always done. Not that I'm going to run out and buy halide lights as soon as I get out so that I can grow immediately; but you know, things were pretty good between us. Why would you want to screw something like that up?

Love Art

Nightcrawlers

———— •——

In the dime store in downtown Bainesville, among the racks of Marvel Comics and tufted troll keychains and the capsules of glow-in-the-dark worms, I felt like a freak. It figured I should feel like a monster in the podunk town where Mom had finally settled after she had taken my brother Dillon and me from the house in Fall City. At least, there, we were near enough to Seattle that even the kinds of guys who played on the football team and wore their letterman's jacket while they played *Tempest* or *Missile Command* had shoulder-length hair. Mom took us so far out that everyone still wore buzz cuts. They didn't even have their own arcade; instead, so many people lined up to play *Donkey Kong* at the truck stop that, unless you had inherited one of the quarters lined up along the plastic rim of the machine, you had no way of getting a turn with Mario.

It was the Sunday before the first day of school and I was waiting at the dime store to meet Wendy. Her mother ran the orchards for my mother's old college friend, Ray Burke. He was the reason Mom came out here in the first place. He owned everything out here. As soon as we arrived, he shipped my brother and me off to work in his apple orchards, I figure so that he could get more time alone with Mom. I don't think he realized he didn't need to go to all that much trouble to bag her.

Right before Wendy showed up, I watched this guy wearing a blue flight jacket and black boots. He had been sitting at the counter, drinking black coffee, eating a donut, and reading the paper. And he was just my age. I dug around in the bottom of my pocket and bought myself a paper and sat at the counter. The old guy who ran the place turned from the grill where he flipped hash browns and omelets. "What's it going to be?"

"Glass of milk."

The guy looked up from his paper. He glanced at me. I felt my ears burn under my long strands of hair just like they did when I used to ride my old motorbike through the winter sleet, and I made up my mind right then to cut all my hair off, even if Wendy said she loved my hair. "No one around here," she said, "has hair like your hair, except me. But not even my hair is as soft as your hair." She let me lay my head in her lap, and I'd just lay there under the apple trees while she stroked my hair and pulled on my sideburns. In the diner, drinking my glass of milk, trying to make out what the hell was going on in the world through the paper, I wanted to have short hair and a real job and be just like these hicks way out where it looked like Mom had finally settled down.

The guy snapped his change down on the counter, folded his paper exactly in half, flipped it under his arm and started walking like he had places to go. I paid for my milk. When I got outside, the guy was halfway down the block. He popped open the door to an old Mustang. Like I said, he was just around my age, and he had a car, and when he started it, he backed right out and then was on his way to wherever he was going.

Wendy was coming down the sidewalk. She had walked
by that guy and he hadn't even glanced at her. He just
kept walking to his car. I noticed how dumpy Wendy could
look sometimes. She had on this black and red plaid skirt
and grey wool sweater that had started to unravel in places,
leaving a few crazy fibers sticking out here and there like
an old wicker laundry basket.

"Hi, Milton," she said. She leaned over and kissed me
on the lips right there on the street and I thought, Jesus,
I guess this is all right. But as we walked over to the Burger
Hut, I couldn't get over the idea of how controlled this
guy had been, drinking his coffee, reading his paper,
minding his own time and driving his own car.

The one thing that really put me off about Wendy was
that her mother, who everyone called Momma Eileen,
hated my mother and my brother Dillon, and I'm sure
that she wasn't too fond of me. My mother lived in Mr.
Burke's best rental house, and because she was a friend
of Mr. Burke, Momma Eileen always asked me questions
about my mother, like "When is your mother going to get
out of this place? Is it true your mother knew Mr. Burke
back in the sixties?"

Momma Eileen seemed as old as anyone I'd ever seen.
Along her jaw, tissue hung in loose sacks, like sandwich
bags filled with water. Beneath the leather cord necklace
that pressed a turquoise amulet to the base of her neck,
her skin turned as smooth and white as a freshly made
bed. Stringent grey hair had long since pushed out most
of her brown hair. Each strand lay stark and almost trans-
parent in the younger hair. Instead of growing old all over,
she had started to lose this or that part like a cheap stereo
at the end of its warranty.

Her denim dresses had been sewn from worn Levi's
jeans. Sometimes she wore a dress that had been made
from a huge flag she had stolen from the Idaho potato

baron, J.R. Simplot, during the only hippie march and riot that Boise ever had. She and six other flower fags had yanked Simplot's fifty-by-eighty-foot flag down, and from the fabric they had made twelve dresses and four shirts. Four days later, they wore them in the Moscow Riot, where every Idaho hippie was busted.

Momma Eileen worked as the foreman of Mr. Burke's upper orchard. She lived in a mess of buildings at the top edge of the field, where the mountain started to rise. Her place had been bunched together, a silver trailer camper welded to the side of a yellow school bus. Once painted rainbow colors, the enamel flaked from the metal.

She wasn't a total hermit, but pretty close. She lived with her three daughters. The oldest daughter, Wilma, believed that her father had been Abbie Hoffman. The middle daughter, Wanda, claimed that her father was Donovan, who I had never heard of, but one night Wanda played me some of her supposed father's records and he sounded folksy and annoying and I didn't know how to get her to turn him off, seeing as how he was her father. Wendy, the youngest daughter, didn't know or really care who her father was, but she told me while we were working apples in late September that if she had to pick a father it would be Mahatma Gandhi. "Momma would have to have used frozen sperm, because he died so long ago." I found Wendy so completely wonderful that when she told me this I fell to the dusty, straw-covered earth and rolled away, laughing so hard I started to cry.

Wendy and I worked in the lower field. Our foreman, Mr. Gidican, liked his crew to work for fifty-five minutes and then take a five-minute break. After work, Wendy brushed her long braid of hair back behind her. She leaned down to help me up. Her wrists, thin and muscular, sprung taught as I yanked her hand. I grabbed her soft upper arm and pulled her down to the ground.

"Thanks," I said, "for helping me up." I kept laughing. I jumped and I hauled her up, but she kicked me in the round fat behind my shin. I howled and followed her down to the road, where I jumped on the bus back to town.

Momma Eileen had caught my brother Dillon. She had never liked him, anyway, because he talked all the time. The poor bastard should get a job as a talker because that's all he does, and it's a pity because for all that talking he doesn't think one bit. A week before, toward the end of the day, Dillon had been picking up windfall apples. He didn't rest at all that day, like he needed to, and then an hour before we had to go down the hill to get on the bus, he took a break. He lay under a tree and fell asleep. Gidican usually came around to check on our crew an hour before closing. He had checked us almost every day since we had started. For all Dillon and I knew this was some sort of rule written down somewhere. It didn't take brains to tell you not to mess with the rules, written or not. But Dillon, because he hadn't taken his breaks, because he hadn't had his water, lay down, his work boots crossed over one another, his hands folded over his stomach. Along came Gidican. He yanked Dillon up by one arm and slapped him in the face, giving him a bloody nose. Lucky Dillon didn't get anything broken. "Don't you sleep on my shift, you spoiled punk. Go to the house and talk to the foreman." Dillon, still being stupid, went to the big house. He lifted the brass knocker where we got paid by Momma Eileen, instead of going to the front where Mom's old college chum, Burke, might have found him. Gidican would have really caught it and Dillon would probably have scored a great job in the packing plant in downtown Bainesville. When Momma Eileen opened the door, she just stared at him holding his Old Faithful of a bleeding nose. "You all right?"

"Can I speak to Mr. Burke?"

"He's not in. Why don't you come inside and I'll get you a bandage." She poured Dillon a straight shot of vodka from the bottle she kept in the rafters. She told him it was medicine and he should drink it down in one gulp. Dillon gulped it down and howled. "What was that?"

"Medicine." She went to get Mr. Burke, leaving Dillon on the bench. He sat there getting woozy and wondering why his nose wasn't hurting anymore. Mr. Burke came downstairs to find my brother completely toasted and with a broken nose. He called my mother and told her that he couldn't have this kind of disruption out in the orchard. "It's dangerous."

Wendy stood on an old wooden chair, green with mold, reaching her hands up into the faint sunlight that arced through the shadows under the cedar trees. She brought me here to show me the face she and her sisters had found at the top of the mountain, back in the canyons behind the town. The face, covered with moss, had been poured from concrete. About the size of a car tire, the wind-rubbed cheeks and flat nose looked like a fat man or woman that had just told a dirty joke; the lips curled back, exposing pebble teeth. Wendy chanted as she swayed on top of the chair. I sat on the dry cedar tree needles and listened and if I felt like joining in I could, but as I sat on the pitchy ground, looking up at her half singing, I started to sing a song my father used to play whenever he played a song. He owned a guitar but this was the only song he ever sang with it:

> *You got to walk that lonesome valley,*
> *You got to go there by yourself,*
> *Ain't nobody here can go there for you,*
> *You got to go there by yourself.*

Wendy stopped rocking on the chair then and hunched down to listen to me. "Where'd you learn that?"

"The radio."

"They don't sing songs like that on the radio."

"Sure they do."

She tackled me and forced my head into the prickly bed of leaves.

"Tell me."

"No." She rolled away from me and looked up at the swaying cedar tree branches. The stand of trees lay at the bottom of a gully. Below us the stream fed a river, and down the river the orchards started. We had all today. Tomorrow we started school. I didn't want to go, but I also wanted to go because Wendy was just a grade ahead of me and I could see her every day in her school clothes instead of the ragged jeans and plaid shirt she wore in the orchards.

"What are you wearing to school tomorrow?" I asked.

"Same thing I always wear on the first day, some dress Momma made this summer. She orders fabric from some-place and sews with the Singer, a new dress in the latest style."

"A handmade dress couldn't possibly be in the latest style," I said, sort of off-hand, not really thinking about the effect this would have on her, but Wendy sat up and jumped onto the chair. Sometimes I'd do something, just haul off and hit my brother and I wasn't sure why I'd done it. It's the stuff I don't mean to do that really gets me in trouble. She raised her hands in the air, closed her eyes, and just rocked back and forth.

"What are you doing?" I asked Wendy. I brushed the needles out of my hair and looked up at her. She barely breathed; she held her eyelids so wrinkled they looked like apples left on a windowsill.

"Quiet," she said.

"I've been quiet,"

"Sssh."

I looked at her long, pale arms raised into the air. I could see the faint map of purple veins underneath her skin. A light blue layer of hair covered her arms. When she hugged herself, her long, knotted fingers left indents in her fleshy upper arms. Like her mother, her hands had already aged years faster than the rest of her. Because she wore a long-sleeve shirt working in the orchard, her old hands stopped at her wrists.

After a long while, she mumbled. "I wish, sometimes, that I was a dryad, one of those tree spirits, because I would like to just be the space right here, where I'm hanging, and feel the sunlight come down against me, and in the winter time, the snow would fall around the outside of me. Deer would come inside me and paw the ground at my roots and eat the lichen growing on my bark."

"I wouldn't want you to be a tree because someone would cut you down."

"No one would even want these trees, they're small and worthless."

"You want to be a worthless tree?"

"I just want to float here, in the middle of this field, with a stream running through my roots, watching the clouds float on by and the winters come and go, and I'll just grow old and old and strong."

"That's what you're doing now."

"I'm sixteen years old. I'm at my peak already and I've just started life. It's all downhill from now. My eyesight'll start to knock out soon and I'll need glasses like Wilma. One day I'll be like Momma. I'll just have stories from the one or two years when I was at my peak. If I were a tree, my peak would be so long it would be stupid to call it a peak. It would just be the way I am."

"That's cool," I said. I kicked the bottom of her chair and she tumbled into the mattress of rotting needles and leaves. I jumped at her and grabbed a handful of the soft, cold skin on the back of her thigh.

She kicked me off her and pulled her dress straight and smiled at me. "Come on," she said, and skipped out into the full sunlight of the field. I followed her, blinking in the hot light, not really able to see anything, just the stark whiteness of the billowy clouds and the hard shadows of the stand of cedar trees.

At school the next day, I went to the bathroom to primp before I found Wendy, when this thing happened. The bathrooms in a new school have always been the one thing that stand out to me, maybe because I've been cornered in so many of them, maybe because it's in the bathroom, in front of the sinks and mirrors where the boys comb their hair and talk and smoke, that I feel completely outside their lives. Though the stories are familiar and I've been involved in some of their plots in the past, the names are always different, and in this bathroom, listening to these boys talk, I didn't know that John had driven off the canyon road, that Jerry's girlfriend was pregnant, that Jason's band had broken up after his mother found out that they were playing taverns.

It could also be the closeness these school bathrooms forced on us. The toilet stall doors had been removed, and sitting on the toilet, staring blankly out at the line of guys primping, I found myself reading and rereading the graffiti. I found that Wilma, Wendy's older sister was the school's resident slut. "For all your vacuuming and sucking needs call Wilma Denty."

"Excuse me," I said, trying to step past a short guy in a plaid shirt with the sleeves rolled up. He wore an ORTHO baseball cap; its tall peak almost made him normal size.

"Back of the line, shit-for-brains."

"Please, I just need to wash my hands, fuck-sneeze."

The guys in residence at the sinks started to laugh. The noise ricocheted off the urinals. ORTHO pulled a switch blade handled comb out of his pocket, the kind that I had carried around with me in fourth grade. The other fourth graders weren't impressed then.

"Jesus, man," I said. "I didn't mean to incite you into a fucking killing frenzy."

"You're a smart ass, you know that?"

"I must be, seeing as I have shit for brains." I waited for him to flick the comb open.

The bathroom door opened. "Sorry, didn't mean to intrude." He closed the door.

ORTHO flicked the lever and a long black comb jumped out of the handle. He made a face at me, and turned back to the mirror, swept off his cap, and combed his hair, as if he didn't even notice me. "You fucking get out of my bathroom before I brutalize your ass."

I grabbed the back of his oily head and just as the door opened again, I brought ORTHO's skull down into the porcelain sink. "There's a fight!" yelled someone outside the bathroom. ORTHO's neck buckled over the wide ledge so that I could bounce his nose on the aluminum drain casing. But the spigot caught on his forehead, digging through his skin and cracking on his skull. His arms flopped against the drain pipes and the other guys in the room just backed away from the line of sinks. I pulled him back and dropped him to the tiles. I rinsed the blood down the drain, dispensed the gritty school soap into my hands, and washed the hair oil from my hands.

My mother believed in cleansing violence. She thought that *Bonnie and Clyde* was a positive example of bloodshed, as if there was something redeeming in Bonnie and Clyde bonding over Tommy guns. I believed, however, that I was brought to my most violent acts, I mean the kind people would think noteworthy, when I couldn't even think and everything happened to me without leaving any imprint at all. I spent the rest of the day comfortable that I would be pulled out of class. I listened to my history teacher tell us the rules of her class. "I do not tolerate foul language." The language arts teacher told us the rules of his class. "This is not a collaborative class. If I catch you cheating, you will flunk." In PE, I couldn't find a gym partner, and because we had an odd number of boys I got to have a locker all to myself. It was only my first day and I had stepped into that total freak zone occupied by the mumblers and pants pissers, the outer margin of outcasts who just can't, for whatever reason, deal with the other kids. A noticeable gap followed me around in the hallways and I knew this fear couldn't be good. And I was never pulled from class, and I never saw Wendy.

After school, I went around to the store and warehouses in Bainesville, filling out job applications so that I could have a job and be a normal kid. At the sporting goods store, I met Mr. Breathe. A sign, written with a black Magic Marker, propped against a stuffed deer and a line of fishing poles in the front display window, read: "Help needed now. Inquire within only if you can start immediately." The sign had yellowed and curled. A spider had spun a line from one edge of the sign up to the deer's antlers, and little knots of dead flies hung from web like dusty Christmas lights. Mr. Breathe sat in a gigantic swivel chair behind the back counter. Behind him, he had almost every bullet for every rifle made after 1880. They were in long drawers, with the caliber and a small drawing printed on the front. Above the wall of bullets, he had a roll-down metal grate. Mr. Breathe wore a red, geometric Navajo sweater. His head was connected to the sweater by a long, curly, red beard that broke into two forks over his stomach. "I'll help you," he said to me when I first stepped into the store, walking down the aisle packed with tents, rain coats, rubber rafts and tent spikes.

"I'm here to apply for the job."

"Job?"

"The sign, 'Ask Inside?'"

Mr. Breathe swiveled and stepped free of his chair. He took a step. The plop of his boot sole sounded like a dropped phone book. Then he took another step forward. Once he had cleared the narrow area behind the counter he hurried to the front of the store. "That's not my handwriting."

"I didn't put it there," I said.

Mr. Breathe began to chuckle. "No. I didn't believe you did. There's a spider web on it. Anyhow, a young man like yourself shouldn't be working."

"My family needs the money."

"You've got kids?"

"A mother and a brother."

"I'm not about to give you a job if all you're looking for is to put wide tires on your car."

"Did you just open?"

"Just open? Stop. Smell." We stood in the middle of the store, under the florescent lights, on the formica tiles, and breathed in the ancient odor of mothballs, long-gone fish, curing venison, and gun oil. "This is not the smell of a store that has just opened. I've been the sole proprietor of Breathe Sporting Goods since 1964."

"Are you hiring?"

"On principle I work alone. Call me a hermit businessman, if you will. But I'm a businessman first. What can you do?"

"You name it, I've done it and would like to do it again. I'll earn you so much money, you'll have to start a chain store just to keep up with the business."

"I do need something, but I don't think a kid like you, with school and all, would enjoy it."

"Anything."

"Can you worm? I'll pay you two cents a worm, up to a thousand worms a day."

"Earthworms?"

"Nightcrawlers. Are you up for that?"

"Only if you can use a million worms a week."

"Twenty bucks for a thousand worms."

"And a real job in a month?"

"And a chance to get hired into the sporting goods business, sure."

We shook hands and I walked off Main Street, down a back alley, and kept to the alleys because I was afraid ORTHO and his friends would be looking for me after school. I didn't know them, though I'd been living in the valley since the summer and had met many people working in the orchards. But all the people I worked with had gone south or to big cities for the winter.

At Momma Eileen's trailer, I knocked on the door until Wendy flung it open. "What?"

"I have a new job."

"Yeah?" She came down the steps and then went back inside the bus and closed the door. I waited on the steps for a long time, and finally she came out with hot caramel apples and her jacket. "How was your first day of school?"

"I've got a normal job," I said.

"Yeah, doing what?"

We ate our apples and walked up the road. "Do you know where I can find nightcrawlers?"

"Fishing? Are you going fishing?"

"I need to find an earthworm orgy. To get a job at Breathe Sporting Goods I have to come up with a thousand earthworms a day."

"Oh yeah, that's a normal job, Milton. Anyway, they're all dead."

I stopped in the middle of the road and took a bite of my caramel apple. I rolled the crisp chuck of apple in my mouth until the soft caramel skin pulled off.

"It's okay, I'm kidding, numbskull, I know where some are." We walked to the shed were Momma Eileen kept her tools, a shovel, a spade, and a ten-gallon paint drum. I followed her across the pasture and then through the thin pine trees to a field that rolled down to a pool of water where a stream came down the hill. Young pine trees spread over the pasture, sticking up out of the wild grass. At the far end, just before the land suddenly jutted up toward the top of the ridge, tottered a dilapidated shack. Wendy walked to the middle of the field, planted the shovel, where she left it sticking up. "Here you are, worm heaven. We used to keep some cows here and this whole field has so much decomposing cow shit that I bet it's seething with worms."

I dug a clod of damp, black soil from the ground, held together with long, yellow grass roots. Just under the sod, dozens of fat nightcrawlers wiggled their heads in the air. I banged the clod against the bucket, filling it with loose bits of earth, gravel, and earthworms. Soon, I had a five foot square of churned-over earth and more than my quota of worms.

"Do you count them?" Wendy asked me. She hunched

down beside the full bucket. She pushed on the side of it with the ball of her hand. "How do you plan on taking this back down?"

"I can lift it," I said. I tried, though, and the bucket's wire snapped off. We left the bucket in the field and went to get the wheelbarrow at Momma Eileen's shed. In the fading daylight, we returned to the field to find hundreds of nightcrawlers dangling over the edge of the bucket, their elastic bodies stretched down into the ground. I held my breath and then scooped up their sticky, rubber-band bodies into the bucket. "How many do you think escaped?"

Wendy asked, "Guess how many earthworms are in this new Oldsmobile, and you can take it home."

I heaved the bucket up from the bottom and set it in the wheelbarrow and began the long walk toward Breathe Sporting Goods store. As we walked out of the hills, past the first houses, a Mustang passed us with its lights on. We walked past the city houses. I think she and I were sort of happy with our catch for the day. I felt this strange sort of energy with her, as if she would help me, no matter what. I had forgotten all about her absence during the school day. Now we were carting out nightcrawlers, right out of the hills, like gold, and we'd get twenty bucks.

At the Breathe Sporting Goods store, the Mustang sped past us, running a red light. Wendy raised her eyebrows. "That was James Dorn." Mr. Breathe sort of slumped off his stool and he sauntered around the end of the counter. "Back so soon?"

"Yes, Mr. Breathe. I have a thousand earth worms, I think."

"You think? How many do you have?"

"To be honest, I have no idea."

"Guess," Wendy said, still on her joke. Mr. Breathe didn't get it, but he was smiling. He came back with a box full of plastic cups with lids that already had holes cut them. "It is six o' clock now. Put fifty worms and a little dirt in each cup, and I'll put you two on the payroll."

"Great," I said.

"Not me," Wendy said.

She watched me as I sorted the earth and dropped the wriggling worms into the cups. After an hour, I had sixteen of them full and had cheated a little so that I could get the sixteenth full enough that he wouldn't notice.

"Great," Mr. Breathe strolled around the table. "Clean up this mess, and I'll cover the remaining two hundred worms and pay you your twenty bucks."

Wendy smiled at me. As soon as we were out of the store, she twirled around. "Who knew?"

"Who knew what?"

"That we could get so much money for so little work?"

"I did the work, that's why."

"For twenty bucks, I'd do the work."

As soon as we stepped out of the store, the red Mustang pulled up and two guys from the bathroom hopped out. "Hey, Wendy," one of them said. "How's Wilma?"

"Are you going to come peaceful or are we going to have to hunt you down?" one of the guys said.

I looked between them to the guy wearing the flight jacket at the wheel of the Mustang. He looked straight into my eyes. I had to look away because I could never stare someone down when I'd stacked the odds so heavily in my own favor. Three against one? I smiled and started to run. I heard them behind me, and then they stopped. "Come back, shit for brains, or we'll beat the shit out of your girlfriend."

I still ran.

I would be a liar if I said I was not afraid of getting beaten up. My knees had that funny electrical feeling like

I got when I used to jump off the tallest trestle over the Snoqualmie River. I mean, there is that fear, but that never stopped me from doing anything. I would get thrashed, fine. But I ran because I was afraid of what I might do to them, I mean, if things got out of hand and they weren't able to grab my arms and hold me down quickly enough. There was all kinds of crap, branches and garbage cans, the kinds of stuff I might get a hold of once I lost it. I could kill someone. So I ran and looked like a coward. My dad always told me that if I got into a fight, I should run to the police station. "It's not your job to beat people up," he said. I always thought he was a little retarded for thinking like this, but in a way I sort of understood now.

After I passed through the alley, I hurled myself across a vacant lot next to the barber shop. Then I hid between two dumpsters at the Burke Co. Building. I don't know. I had been beat up enough as a young kid and I don't think I wanted any more of it. How often did I have to get beat up?

Minutes later, the two guys ran out into the middle of the vacant lot and then looked around. The guy driving the car must've grabbed Wendy, but they knew her and I didn't think they would actually hurt her.

While I waited at the dumpster it started to rain, and then, hours later, I began to walk back to Momma Eileen's house, to see if Wendy had come home. I watched for the two guys. It was almost completely dark along the road. As I came up the steep side of the hill, I heard a car coming, and I climbed down into the pitch dark pasture on the side of the road. I waded into the rushing ditch and up onto the soggy ground. The car lights filled the air with a silvery glow and all around me I saw earthworms wriggling out of the ground. I had never really thought about earthworms before. I supposed they were in the ground and as common in the earth as bugs are in the air. But I didn't really think about them when I walked over the ground. And there were hundreds of them under there, wriggling and living their worm lives. I remembered from school that an earthworm had both sex organs. I supposed it must be lonely to have both and be blind. You'd have children for whom you'd be both the mother and father, children you'd never seen.

The car turned down the road and I hurried up the hill. At the top of the hill, I could see the Mustang parked in front of the trailer. One of the boys who'd chased me was sitting in the front seat and Wendy was in the other seat and Momma Eileen and Wilma were standing under the porch light, holding up a gigantic umbrella that wasn't doing any good because the rain was blowing down sideways.

"He's just a loser I hang out with," I heard Wendy say. "I didn't know what he did."

"If he can do something like that," Momma Eileen said. "I don't think I want you hanging around him."

"And his breath always smells," Wilma said. The guys in the car laughed. I wiggled back into the bank and listened to them.

"He just left me standing in front of that store, running like a coward," Wendy said. "I thought he had more fight in him than that."

"He's a vicious coward and we won't rest until he's taken down," one of the boys said.

"Hell, yes," one said.

I slid down the slope and I felt empty. All around me I could hear the rain falling in the darkness and I knew that seething in the ground were hundreds of thousands of earthworms. I didn't want anyone to see me. I didn't want to exist. I wanted to be with Wendy in that stand of cedar trees, just her and me and the sunlight and wind pushing through that space, just the two of us, growing old, old and strong.

The House Below

Laughing Horse Reservoir

———◆———

When the boys and I moved into the house Ray Burke provided for us at the end of the dirt road above Bainesville, the last tenants were still packing their things into a Ford pick-up truck. Boils of rust spread from the tire rims. The paint had long since faded and worn to what must have been the primary color of all cars, the scoured tint of a second-hand teaspoon's dish. In contrast, I felt like a movie star wearing my sunglasses in my husband's Supersport Impala convertible as I watched my two almost grown sons jump out of the car and immediately claim the porch of the house. The children of the evicted tenants cowered at the edge of the stairs behind boxes of blankets and plates.

I knew Ray Burke from the time I had dropped out of college, before I had even met my ex-husband, Art. Ray and I had hung around the same people in Seattle in the mid-sixties. Fifteen years later, he still mailed the odd letter or Christmas card to Mom's address. Now, retreating East away from my mother and my husband, I had followed the return address on Ray's last card all the way to Bainesville. Ray had drawn Magic Marker blue smoke trailing from Archangel Gabriel's trumpet, transforming it into a huge hash pipe. Gabriel had been foil stamped onto handmade paper; the odd mix of middle school humor and class was classic Ray.

When I knocked at his family's old house, he slammed open the door and grabbed me, hugging me in his loose-armed way where he just left his arms on my shoulders. He cried a little. I noticed a faint sound coming from deep inside him like the whimper of a puppy locked in a box. He wore the same black T-shirt, blue jeans, and stupid grin he had worn years ago. "You haven't changed," I said. "It's great to see you."

"Not a day older," he said.

Around the house he had rented to me, the second-growth pine leaned into the hot August sky. The small pasture, the swampy field across the road, and the bright green propane tank, everything, seemed a little too perfect. Nothing was ostentatious about the place—its bubbled wainscotting had to be at least fifty years old—but the steep roof, the lack of any neighbors whatsoever was too good. Everything was ideal except the family Ray had displaced in his incredibly huge welcome to me, a minor character in a crowded scene from his past. Maybe it was because I was the only person in this entire valley who remembered him from before he owned the biggest farm, the apple orchards, the range land, and even the packing plant. I was the only person in on the joke of how ridiculous it was that an old hippie like him was in charge.

The evicted father smiled and pumped Ray's hand. The man wore a white T-shirt that swelled over his extended belly. His thin legs were as thin as two frayed garden hoses. "How do you do, Mr. Burke?" He bowed slightly, keeping his mouth cracked in a wide grin over his square teeth. He didn't even glance at me. His wife, who was pretty and brown and pregnant, already sat in the truck. She brushed a lock of black hair away from her eyes. The gear knob rose between her knees like a rubber knobbed flower. The three smallest kids sat next to her. The two older boys sat on top of the tightly packed boxes and furniture heaped in the truck bed.

"How do you do, John?" Ray grabbed John by the neck and said something into his ear.

"Please forgive me for the time it took to pack. Sudden notice and all. I had to pack all the kitchen things. I had to drag the kids out of their rooms. I had to trap the cats and pack them up in cardboard boxes." He said this to me and smiled and shook his head. "You don't know good memory until you tell your kids to find their toys in a hurry."

"Let's check it out," Ray said. "Let's see how you left the place."

A sofa sat in the living room, kittywampus to the wall. I didn't know how old the sofa was but the fibers had started to unravel like a gigantic ball of yarn. "You're not leaving this here, are you?"

"What? You don't want the sofa?" John asked.

"I don't think so, John," Ray said.

"I'll take it, Mr. Burke. I'm very glad to keep it. My entire family has grown up on this sofa. My two youngest children were born right in this room on this sofa in the winter of '79 and '80. Both terrible winters. If they can't grow up in this house, then they'll have the sofa they were born on. But I have to be honest with you, Mr. Burke, this was your sofa."

"Look, John, you'll take it with you. Boys, give him a hand." Ray didn't move to help Dillon and Milton lift the couch. "Let's check the rest of the house for anything you might have left behind."

They walked up the stairs, leaving my sons to struggle with the sofa. "Lift with your legs," I said, but already Milton hefted the couch up. Milton angled it up so that the weight pushed down on Dillon.

"Heh," Dillon said, and dropped the couch. The house shook and the windows tittered.

"Watch the hardwood floors," Ray called from upstairs.

"Keep it up, or you're a pansy," Milton said to Dillon. They staggered across the room. Milton's face started to get red and as bright as the coil of the Supersport's cigarette lighter. "Don't make me carry the whole thing."

Dillon tried to hurry out the front door, through the tight space of the landing. The sofa didn't quite fit through the first door frame, but the boys struggled and turned it and finally moved it through the door, leaving deep gouges in the soft layers of enamel coating the frame. The second door was even more narrow. Milton kept pushing and Dillon pulled. Finally a hollow crack ripped out of the sofa and it slid through the two door frames like a Kleenex coming out of its box. The back of the couch had gone limp, but Milton pushed the sofa into Dillon and Dillon had to run across the lawn to keep from falling. Finally he tripped and the whole thing landed on him. "It's broken," he said.

"It's not," Milton said.

"Toss that thing in the truck," Ray yelled from an upstairs window.

"Let me help," John called.

"There's not enough room," Milton said.

"Move those boxes out of the truck," Ray yelled, again.

Milton jumped up into the truck and handed the first box to Dillon. Dillon reached up and then his entire body followed the box down into the grass. The box landed solidly on the ground. He lay next to it for a second and then slowly hauled himself up and stood with his hands on his knees, swaying a little.

"Let me help," I said.

Milton started hurling the boxes onto the lawn. Dillon asked him to hand him the ones with glass in them. "How can I tell if they have glass in them?" He kept throwing the boxes out.

Dillon rushed around and checked the fallen boxes. "This one had glass in it."

"You're such a dick, Stickbutt."

"Milton, get off that truck now, and go inside. I told you not to call him Stickbutt anymore." Milton used to call Dillon Stickbutt all the time. At first it had been sort of affectionate. He'd say "Can Stickbutt come with me?" But then it turned into this thing where he'd ride Dillon until Dillon tried to hit him and then he'd wrestle Dillon to the ground and rub his face with mud and dirt.

"You can slow down," I said.

Milton didn't stop throwing the boxes out. "I'm almost done."

John came out onto the porch carrying a box of green and brown beer bottles. He stood next to me, sweating long rivulets that had plastered his T-shirt into two patches under what I can only call his breasts. Wiping his forehead with the back of his hand, he looked at me. "There's no rush." That didn't slow Milton down.

When he'd thrown out the last box Milton asked Ray, "So should we toss the couch in? You'll have to help me because Dillon isn't strong enough."

Ray rolled up his sleeves and they hauled the couch into the bed of the truck. It barely fit, so they propped it up on the tailgate. When they were done, Ray said, "I need a glass of water," and went inside and Milton followed him.

I helped John and his wife look through the boxes. The water glasses had survived, but a box of large brown ceramic plates had landed on a fist-sized stone, cracking every plate. They packed the box with the rest of their things. "Thank you," John said. "I appreciate your help." He climbed into the truck.

Ray slammed the door behind him. He circled me with one arm around my shoulders and squeezed me to him. "Hey, John, see you at the house Monday morning? A lot needs to be done."

"Sure thing, Mr. Burke," he said.

Ray hugged me and said, "Sorry. They were supposed to be gone already."

John's two oldest boys, still several years younger than Dillon, climbed up onto the pile of loosely secured furniture in the back of the pick-up and waved at me and the house where they had been living as they drove away.

As the truck rolled down the tar-and-gravel road along the river toward Bainesville, I noticed a sort of white noise had vanished and I could hear the leaves in the poplars across the road. The wallpaper remained dark in the places where their furniture had been, and the rest of the wall had bleached from pale green to almost white. Dust lay on top of the fresh, healthy squares of carpet where cabinets and the fruit-crate bookcases had been. There should have been more indications of the family's life in the old building. The empty walls and dust balls didn't say much about the people who had just been living in the space. I didn't know how long they had been here. Walking through the empty rooms, I attempted to remember the houses where I had lived when I was a child, but I hardly recalled the cities where I had lived, much less the homes or rooms. As a child, the furniture had remained constant but the houses had retained the alien odor of the previous tenants' cooking even after my father had polished the bookcases with the antique wood oil he ordered from the back of the *Smithsonian*. With each move, I expected to arrive at a better life instead of weekday meals of hot dog slices floating in a macaroni-and-cheese bath and a bowl of canned peaches. Whenever we moved to a new house my parents filled it with the familiar old furniture and soon the familiar old arguments started again.

The kitchen had plenty of room to store anything I wanted to eat. A streamlined fifties Frigidair squatted in a corner of the room. Tall cupboards with beveled glass panes and a narrow two-burner gas range packed the rest of the kitchen. The entire house matched the description of my ideal place, something Ray and I had discussed almost twenty years before. The living room looked over the valley and the back windows looked into a backyard stuffed with knots of wild grass and patches of broken brown glass and a fire pit with the charred remains of Budweiser cases. Beyond the yard, the columns of second-growth pine grew sparsely enough that foxglove and daisies grew between the gray trunks.

On the back landing, I found a homemade doll that the previous tenant's kids might have left. Bushy hair grew out of a stuffed ball anchored to a burlap potato-sack body. It wore a denim patch for a vest and two long seams defined its toes at the end of overstuffed legs. I realized then that someone had spent a long time working on the head. What had seemed like haphazard sewing had created a face that reminded me of Ray. The doll had the same cleft chin and pinched eyebrows. A long knitting needle skewered the doll almost through the middle of its chest but a little off to the left. One of its black button eyes had come off. From the hole, cotton stuffing spilled loose. I tried to push the white fluff back but the minute threads caught a hang-nail and I drug out a thin line of cotton.

"What do you have there?" Ray pressed my body into the wall of the narrow hall.

"One of the kids left this doll behind."

"It will give them a chance to make a new one. By the looks of this one, they'll need as much practice as they can get." Ray laughed.

He held the doll in his hand, and I looked from the doll's face to Ray's face. "It looks just like you. A Voodoo Ray Doll. Doesn't everyone you ever knew carry one of these?"

"It doesn't look like me. Why do you have to say things like that?" I followed him through the house until he stopped in front of the mirror in the bathroom. His fingers combed back his hair. He stood straight and turned to squint at himself. He caught me standing in the hallway, watching him. "I don't look anything like that doll."

"We should take it back to them."

"If they wanted it, they would have kept it. Besides, maybe someone left it here before they lived here? It could belong with the house. Really, I'm pretty sure it belongs to the place. Any of the old tenants could have left it. A lot of stuff has happened here."

"How old can this place be, Ray? We should take the doll back to them."

"They can get a new one. We all know we wanted a G.I. Joe or Barbie even if our parents stuck us with handmade garbage like this."

"Maybe they can't afford G.I. Joe or Barbie?"

"How much does a fucking Barbie cost?"

"You know, Ray, you have changed."

He thought that was hilarious. "Sure I've changed. But you haven't. Shit, you look great."

He sat on the tub. "I wish I had never gotten involved in owning anything. I was in Moscow a couple of weeks back and in the parking lot of the truck stop, I stopped to listen to these three kids playing guitar while they sat on the fender of a black van with cheesy Beat *Bartlett's Quotation* sayings hand-painted on the sides. 'The only people for me are the mad ones, the ones who are mad to live, mad to talk, mad to be saved,' yadda yadda yadda ending with 'you see the blue centerlight pop and everybody goes "Awww!"'" Ray smiled.

"I'm too old for that sentimental crap now. It's patently ridiculous for people to run around shoving their hearts in people's faces. That is old age. I mean, let's face it, that doll looks a hell of a lot better than me. I've got the worst case of mid-life bloat I ever seen."

I hadn't seen Ray since the summer of 1967, after the spring when he had been pretending to go to classes at the University of Washington. While listening to the second side of *The Doors* album over and over again and staring into a wrinkled Camel wrapper after dropping an eyedropper of lysergic acid, Ray had a vision about an electric guitar, the second coming, and uniting everyone across the globe for a massive, communal bong-a-thon. He had this startling vision on Valentine's Day and by the first day of Spring he could play four chords and holler reasonably well into a microphone. He and several like-minded dropouts started to cover old blues songs. Sometimes they would slip their own material between "Walking Blues" and "Baby, Please Don't Go" and then the sailors and longshoremen, the prostitutes and dealers would slip into the alley behind the saloon where the band had managed to get a permanent gig. People would crowd the bartender. When Ray would belt out the Jim Morrison version of "Backdoor Man," the bar crowd would slip back onto the floor.

The bartender had encouraged them to play their songs. "You know, they're heavy and I don't think they're for everybody, but it gives the patrons time to refresh their drinks. I really like the long number where you're all on that groove and then you start to scream at the end. Real cool."

When Ray received his draft notice, he just disappeared, which wasn't odd at the time. People disappeared almost everyday. They would either get drafted, and then actually go to The War, or they would leave for Canada. Years later, long after I had met Art and had kids, and was working in Fall City, I received a letter from Ray telling me about his adventures and how he had left Seattle for his Dad's orchards in Idaho. His Dad had looked at his draft notice and thrown it into the kitchen oven. "It's settled. I have a little farm in Canada that needs better care than the tenants are giving it." Ray turned the farm around and concentrated his crop on cucumbers and zucchini and became the largest organic supplier in North America.

Ray came back from his car with a case of Olympia beer and a tub of fried chicken from the deli in downtown Bainesville. "Welcome to the new house," he said. He sat in the middle of the hardwood floor. Milton and Dillon squatted down next to him. He passed out paper plates. I stood at the window, looking out at the tops of the fir trees. The timberland stretched for miles. The mountain behind the house rose steeply to the Laughing Horse Reservoir.

"Mom?" Milton asked. He held up an open beer can.

I glanced quickly at Dillon. He didn't have a beer can. Ray had suddenly become very interested in distributing the chicken.

"You like white or dark meat, Janice?"

"Dark. Milton, do you even want me to respond to your question?"

"I am asking."

"Do what you will, you're fifteen now."

"Sounds like yes to me," Ray said.

Milton laughed. "Come on, Stickbutt, drink up."

Dillon pulled a can out from behind his back and opened it up. We watched as Milton drank a long drink, like he hadn't had a drink in months. Milton wiped his lips; his eyes were squinted from the bitter flavor. He set the can down. "So fine," he said.

Dillon took a small swallow and then set his down. I sat on the hard floor with Ray. We all silently ate and sipped beer. "This is good chicken," I said to Ray.

"Bainesville's finest deli," he said.

"You own that too, Mr. Burke?" Milton asked

"Call me Ray," he said. "What do you say after we finish eating I take the boys out and show them the acreage while you get set up?"

"That sounds really nice," I said.

Milton finished his beer and reached for another one.

"Don't you think that sounds fun, Milton?"

"Heh?" he said. He slipped back, letting the can roll

back into the case.

"Don't you think that sounds like it would be fun?"

"Yeah sure. Can I have another beer?"

They came back toward dusk, the three of them laughing and shouting. I didn't know this when they left but Ray had taken a twenty-two caliber rifle with them and they had shot a pheasant. Milton insisted on calling the bird a peasant. "We shot a peasant," he said. "A peasant's a person," I said. "Well, we shot one," he said. They cleaned the bird, wrapped it in tin foil, and left it in the empty freezer. "As soon as I get a chance, I'll be back over to cook it up with your boys," Ray said.

Ray didn't come by to cook up the bird, but we saw each other a lot and the days settled into a routine before I was really certain that I even wanted to stay in Bainesville. Ray found me a job at a truck stop thirty miles down the valley highway, pouring coffee for truckers. I started work late in the afternoon after a long day sun-bathing in the quiet woods or playing records and reading in the living room while the kids were out in Ray's orchards working against the first frosts. The house remained clean and during the day I was bored and happy. At night I chewed gum and talked to the truckers while the warm summer air hung heavy in the parking lot under the false daylight from the nests of arc-lights perched on long steel poles.

One Sunday, at home in the kitchen, drinking a glass of water from one of the green plastic cups that tasted faintly of rubber and the hard mineral soil, I wanted to fill my head with enough marijuana smoke that everything would slow down.

I opened the door and smelled the pitchy odor of the pine trees. I looked back at the house and it looked like a comfortable place in the middle of the clearing with the gravel road gently curling up to its front porch. I walked into the sparse forest, examining everything. The flat lichen-covered stones housed a colony of black ants that hurried to pull their capsule-shaped eggs into their tunnels. I ran my hand over the grooved bark of the pine trees. My hand smelled like matchsticks. In a space where the boughs thinned enough that broken sunlight lit the forest floor and the grass covered earth, I lay down and stared up through the branches into the clear Montana sky, or was it Idaho, or Canada? I didn't know. But lying down, I felt drowsy in the scent of sun-heated rabbitbrush and thistles.

Lying in the hot, loose soil in the middle of the pine forest I wished that I could just be one of the plants, foxglove or a knot of yellow daisies. Dope was a way for me to sort of loosen myself from my duty and life as a mother, even the stress of being a waitress; it stripped me down to skin and nerves and all that mattered was the smooth texture of a glass window pane or the minute variations in the shadow of a telephone pole; all that mattered when I was stoned was the contrast between one moment and the next, the slippage of seconds, which normally trickled by as constant as a dripping faucet into a bathtub.

Dillon once brought home a pamphlet called "Straight Talk About Drug Use." He left it in the tin pan Art used to roll his weed. After work that evening, I scooted the pan out from under the couch and found the pamphlet. I rolled a joint and smoked it while I looked through the booklet. It certainly was straight talk. According to this bit of literature, drugs were pushed by older kids as a sort of initiation rite. The drugs themselves had unpleasant and somewhat gruesome effects that no straight person would want to undergo. The booklet failed to recognize how secretly entertaining marijuana was. When I first smoked it, my friends and I had been talking about it since Monday. Jill's older brother worked as a longshoreman and didn't mind buying vodka for us. He sold her a joint for a dollar; we marveled at how cheap that was. We thought, maybe it doesn't do that much. All week we made stupid jokes about being Beatnicks. "Hey, man," asking for a pencil in study hall, "could you slip me that graphite jam tool?" Friday, at dusk, we met at the elementary school and climbed into the big cement playground pipes and lay against the cool walls, coughing and wheezing on our first bone. "You're not holding it in," Jill said. "James showed me how to do it," and soon we had slipped into that comfortable space where we weren't responsible for our bodies and one thing did not necessarily follow the next.

The little booklet described the weed-induced paranoia as being so intense it would cause people to completely drop out of society, and I suppose with Art that had been the case. He didn't like policemen and would mutter "pig" under his breath whenever he saw a cop. His overall paranoia, what he thought of as his calculated act of civil disobedience, had more to do with his addiction than with any political stance. I guess, toward the end of my marriage with him, that was how I felt about our whole back-to-the-earth thing. I worked as a waitress, for Christsakes, flipping hamburgers created from an animal whose collective ass pumped enough methane into the air to raise global temperatures; everything that we did seemed geared toward supporting Art's comfortable isolation, a secure place for him to get utterly fried.

Coming back to the little house, I realized that I had spent a good deal of the morning out wandering in the forest. I made up my mind that I was going to get high. I didn't go into the house but started the Impala. My personal deal was I would drive until I found a gas station or a church. At the gas station I would ask where I could get some pot and I would forget about the church. At the church, I would sit through the service and forget about the pot.

About four miles down the road, where the gravel joined a paved residential road, stood a small church with a big lot. I drove right past it and told myself that the deal had been weighted too heavily toward the church. A little community like this would be top heavy in churches. If I had been in Seattle, I'd have run into a source more quickly than a church and I'd have, in all fairness, tried to give God another chance.

Another two miles down the road, I came to a second church, a long hall with a tall steeple. A few cars were already in the lot. I parked, put on my sunglasses, and walked into the old place. The electric space-heated air smelled like stale coffee and fungus. The mildewed carpet, the fake oak veneer side panels, the thicket of hardened cobwebs in the rafters were familiar from my mother's occasional bouts of religion. A few older women sat in pews toward the front. Over the church entrance, a back-lit picture of Jesus glowed benevolently across the entire congregation. His hair was slicked back and fell to his shoulder in greasy biker locks. I grabbed a typewritten schedule for the sermon. I paged through the paperback chorus books and settled down in the hard pew wishing I had found the trace of a dealer.

Finally the pastor made his entrance. His coterie of old women shook his hand and helped him across the room and up onto the podium. He took his place, adjusted his papers like a college professor and spoke about the world as a temporal and borrowed place. "You are all here for a brief transition in the complete life of your immortal soul.

You pass through this place like visitors in an old inn, and have the people that were here before cleaned up? Have they left the rooms in a decent condition for your visiting soul?"

After the sermon, an older woman in a yellow sweater with thick sunflowers knitted into a floral breast plate, clasped her hand on the crook of my arm. "How do you do?" she asked. "My name's Marigold Greer."

"How are you?" I asked.

"Excellent," she said. She stared into the air in front of her and when she said this, and then nodded her head confirming her answer and looked back at me. "Just excellent. Where have you driven in from?"

"I live at the end of Mason Road."

"At the Greer farm? Ray Burke owns the place?"

"Yes," I said.

"I used to live there," she said. "I am a Greer."

She drifted away and joined the line of people at the desert table. I followed her through the line, but she kept one step ahead of me. Finally I cornered her outside, chewing on a brownie and washing it down with a cup of weak, lukewarm coffee. We found ourselves alone on the bench by the tire swing outside the Sunday school, in the warm afternoon heat. "We all know about you, you know," Mrs. Greer said. "Mr. Burke has done all this before." Mrs. Greer glanced around, suddenly aware that we were both outside, alone. Her hand shook as she teetered the china cup to her grey lips.

"Before that family lived up in the house, a woman Mr. Burke had met in Rock Springs lived there. One night she ran along the back road and threw herself into the Laughing Horse Reservoir. After they pulled her from the water, a hunter said he had seen her running through the early morning woods, just a flash of white nightgown and her blue feet. That is the part that always gets my thoughts turning. Have you ever gone walking through the woods without your shoes on? It's difficult. But once you get into this way of thinking, you hop over the sharp branches, the briars, and nettles almost like you've become a jackrabbit or something. And it's very pleasant. Each bush, each tree bough becomes a complete living thing. I feel the little ridge that runs down the center of each pine needle. I feel each one as it brushes my face and my arms. This girl was doing all this on the way to the water to drown herself! What grief. The hunter who saw her thought he was dreaming because the woman waved at him and laughed. 'Hey good looking,' she called out to him. The next time he saw her, she was real and in *The Bainesville Chronicle*, a photo some editor had copied out of her high school yearbook."

We stared into the trees, and I imagined this woman Ray had brought to the little house in the forest. I felt the solidity of the house, the security I had felt listening to the rain rattle and roll off the roof, fade then. It was a borrowed place, and I had forgotten how far I had come since leaving Art in Soap Lake.

"I live in an apartment in downtown Bainesville now," Marigold Greer said, "in the place that used to be the only hotel back in the gold rush. We had a gold rush here. Lasted about a year and a half. Well, the business from the rush lasted a year and a half. Reb Hawkins's old goat passed a nugget the size of an apple. When the prospectors figured out that the rush was blown out of proportion they stuck around anyway and Bainesville was a good-sized town for many years. We never did get a railroad spur, so we just died." She took a sip of coffee and grimaced. "Cold coffee I can't stand. I grew up in that house. I learned to swim in that little lake that they've turned into the reservoir. My father built that house when he moved out from Ohio before I was born. Nice place, don't you think? He did a real fine job. Someday, I'd like to ask Mr. Burke to let me just sit in it for awhile. It's been a long time since I've lived there. Long time. A peaceful place, don't you think?"

"It is," I said.

"Excuse me," Mrs. Greer said. "But I'll be needing to return your plates to the kitchen." She stood and absently took my cup. She turned to me and extended her hand. I quickly grabbed it, not shaking it, but just feeling its weight in my hand. "Nice to meet you. "

"Do you know, Mrs. Greer, if you would like, I don't have any plans this afternoon. If you're free you could come over and have some coffee and sit in the living room of the house."

"Are you asking me over for a visit?"

"Would you like to sit in the living room of the house where you grew up?"

"Well, the opportunity presents itself and I don't know."

"Why don't you decide, on the way to my house."

"I'll have to get my umbrella."

When the men came out of the pews they stood directly behind their women, hands guiding wives by their elbows. When the children, excited to be outside, started to speak in loud voices, their fathers issued commands for them to wait in the cars while they gathered under the trees to smoke. I knew a couple of these men from the truck stop but here I could tell from their stiff backs and sloping shoulders that they were with their families. The fathers stood in a group under a sagging hemlock. They wore faint baby blue or green or yellow dress slacks, the polyester cut rough enough that it caught the sunlight coming down like shattered glass. One man, wearing a ragged cowboy hat, cupped his cigarette into the palm of his hand. He stared at me and glanced at Mrs. Greer. He said something and they all darted their eyes toward me and laughed. I ushered Mrs. Greer into the passenger bucket seat. She buckled her seat belt and lay her umbrella across her lap.

She tapped the window with the hard crook of her pointer finger. "That's my Mercury Comet. You'll drop me off back here, won't you? Those men are laughing at you, you know."

"I assumed that. But I've had problems with being too paranoid. That kind of stuff just slips off my back." Really, I wondered how quickly Ray would turn me into one of the wives waiting in the passenger seat of a parked sedan.

"That's what I'm taking about. Spending too much time on your back. A man only knows you for three things." Mrs. Greer coughed and covered her mouth with her fingers. Her nails had been sheared so short that not even the white tips of them showed. She talked through her fingers. "He wants an ear hole to hold every little thought that crosses his mind, a water hole where he can drop his dirty dishes and they'll come out clean, and a knot hole where the can spend himself." She folded her hand around the curved end of her umbrella and looked out the window.

I tried to smile, but she wasn't even looking at me. I just drove along for awhile. "That's a real nice way of putting it," I finally said. When we pulled up the house, I caught myself hoping that Dillon and Milton would be gone.

"It hasn't changed, really. The wall paper's different. My father lay down a real cheap carpet over these hardwood floors, but its all pretty much the same as I remember it."

Mrs. Greer ran her hand down the front of the refrigerator. "This is the fridge my father bought six months before his death. He sold his Pontiac to a collector in Walla Walla and came home with this brand new refrigerator. He had two ice trays. He set them inside the freezer here, and we all sat and talked and talked. He used to tell long stories, let me tell you, and they only had a lick of truth. And finally he opened the thing up and those trays had ice cubes. It sure seemed like something then."

My boiling pan of water started to roll with large bubbles. I slopped water into two mugs and dropped in tea bags.

"It's very nice of you to let me see the place again. Funny thing, you know. I remember every detail of this place. I wonder if you will remember it, you know?"

"I don't think so," I said. "I didn't grow up here."

"You remember your childhood home. You'd go back in a second. You would."

"I don't think I'd like to go back."

"When you get to be my age, you'll want to go back. But I think if you actually had the chance, I don't think you would because there's all that life between. If I could skip the bad bits, just pass into a coma or something like that when it got too tough, I'd go back."

"So, tell me about the woman Ray had stashed here."

"You know, Mr. Burke would never let me come here. I've been asking him for years. Upstairs, there's a cabinet." Marigold Greer set her tea cup on the edge of the counter, and set her purse, a triangle of Naugahyde, in the middle of her lap. She started taking out things, her worn leather glasses case, a silver tube of lipstick, a creased and folded airline ticket, and finally a long metal key with a piece of faded red ribbon knotted around the handle. "You know, this opens the cabinet in the attic."

I waited for her to tell what was there, but she didn't. She took another drink of tea and smiled at me. "Thank you for letting me come over."

"Are you going to open the cabinet."

"I might, but I don't remember what's inside it. What if it's nothing. I didn't expect I'd ever get the chance get to it. Which is silly because I carry this key around."

"Well, today's your lucky day. If it's gold bullion, though, I get a cut."

"Fifty-fifty." Marigold Greer laughed.

I followed her up the stairs, and she asked me to move a rusted aluminum coat rack. A dozen old coats clung to it. I pushed it aside, and against the wall. Flush to the surface, I could see the faint outline of the cabinet under a layer of paint. Someone had puttied in the key hole.

I took a jacket down and removed the wire hanger. I unfastened it, and used the thin point of the wire to loosen the plaster plug from the key hole. Mrs. Greer inserted the key and turned the lock. It snapped free but the door was still shut under layers of old paint.

"Oh damn," Marigold Greer said. "It figures it wouldn't open after all of these years."

"I can try to pry it open," I said.

"You can try, but it's really no use. Just being in the house is good enough."

"We have to open it now," I said. We stopped to listen to the driveway gravel crush under car wheels. "Someone's here," I said.

"We don't have to open it," Marigold Greer said. "But I do want my key back. I'll leave the cabinet unlocked in case you ever want to open it."

As Mrs. Greer and I walked down the attic steps the front door stood open. Ray came out of the kitchen with a beer bottle. He watched as I helped Mrs. Greer down the last step. "Hey," he said. "You have company." He set the beer bottle on the floor and followed us outside. "Mrs. Greer, now I suppose you didn't tell Janice that I told you not to come around here. My father bought his land from your father. The deal is done." Ray turned to me. "Why'd you let this old lunatic here. What's she told you?"

"Nothing, Ray. I ran into her at church,"

"Janice Graham in church? That's horse shit."

"And I invited her to come over and have some coffee and sit in the living room. She grew up here, you know?"

"Yeah, I know. Is that all she told you?"

Milton ran from out of the woods where he'd been playing, building something or more likely burning something. "Hey, Mr. Burke," he said.

"I told her about Amanda, Mr. Burke. I also told her about growing up here."

"Janice, it's blown out of size. No one knows that she lived here with her boyfriend."

"Her boyfriend was you, Mr.Burke."

"It's all very confusing, Ray. Anyway it's your past and I don't really care much about that. God knows I've got one."

"This man has several, Mrs. Graham."

"Mrs. Greer, I've told you several times that if I caught you snooping around the house, I'd call the sheriff," Ray said.

"I grew up here, Mr. Burke. I have some entitlement to visit, especially if I'm invited."

"You are not entitled to anything on this property. Come on with me."

"Ray, I can have whomever I want visiting me."

"It's my house."

"Mom, you should listen to him. Do you know this lady? She looks crazy to me." Milton sat on the porch, twisting a long braid of grass around his middle finger.

"Your son is right, Janice. Do you even know this woman?"

"You're listening to Milton? Who's crazy here? Ray, you're not hearing me."

"I'll take her home."

"When she's ready to leave."

"Janice, this isn't Seattle, for christsakes. You'll take Mrs. Greer off my property, or I swear I'll do something drastic."

"No need," Mrs. Greer said. "I was just leaving."

"You can stay here with Milton until I get back. You left a couple of beers in the fridge, unless Milton's drunk them. But he wouldn't drink his buddy's beer, now would he?"

"You drank them," Milton said.

"I found one," Ray said.

Mrs. Greer clutched her umbrella and followed me back to the Impala. "I'm sorry," she said. "I didn't know he'd be so mad. I once asked that girl who lived her if I could come over, and Mr. Burke himself called and said I should never come to the house."

"Well, I invited you," I said.

When I returned home, no one was in the house. I could hear the poplars across the street swaying in the wind that picked up in the late afternoon. "Dillon?" There wasn't a sound except the constant, almost mute creak of expanding and contracting floor boards, the flap of a jagged tear in one of the conglomerate roof shakes. We had arrived here without a stick of furniture and I had gradually acquired eight pieces from the second-hand store in Bainesville and the Goodwill in Moscow, but still most of the rooms only had a chair.

In Milton's room I could tell that we were just visitors. I hadn't made this place a home. Which didn't help return Milton from the months when he had run away. Milton said he liked his sleeping bag. His bedroll lay over a blanket spread over a mat of cardboard boxes. He kept his things packed into a fruit crate and his frame backpack propped against the wall. The rest of the room was empty. The floors were dusty near the walls. In the far corner, an apple core had lain long enough to grow a beard. I looked through his things, a motorcycle magazine, a half-sized tool box with metallic space-age tape clotted around the screwdriver handles, a battered, portable cassette player, some cassettes without labels, a couple of studio cassettes of bands I had faintly heard of somewhere, maybe just from reading spray-painted bridges: AC/DC, Def Lepard, Iron Maiden, Judas Priest.

"Mom, this is my stuff." Milton squatted down and started arranging his things back into whatever order he had them.

"I was just seeing what you had."

"Are you looking for drugs? Because I don't do that shit. It makes you stupid." Milton grabbed the cassette out of my hand.

"I thought we'd have a big family dinner together, you, Dillon, me and Ray."

"He left because he was so mad about that woman. You shouldn't force anything on him, Mom. You'll just fuck it up. You always do."

"That's not true. I've had a great many successful relationships."

"When?"

"Before you were born." I picked up one of his cassette cases and looked at the Civil War cannon printed on the cover.

"You're not with any of them. You're not even with Dad."

"I didn't mess that one up."

"Someone did."

I looked at Milton. I tried to run my hand through his hair. I suppose he was trying to have the kind of conversation I would have had with him if he was running through girlfriends.

"I think one person who wants to make it work can make it work," Milton said.

"That's a mouthful for a fifteen-year-old kid. I'll call Ray and he'll be glad to come for dinner. You want me to do that?"

"He comes by enough without you asking him."

"I want this time to be special. Formal and nice."

"Fine," Milton said. He grabbed his jacket off the back of the chair and hurried down the stairs. I listened to his body crash into the wall at the bottom of the stair and then the deep thud of the front door slamming closed.

Ray's phone rang and rang and finally he answered breathless and cursing. "What is it?" He said he had been outside playing baseball and drinking. "Excuse me, I'm a little drunk. This is Janice?"

"Ray?"

"Janice, how're you? How come you're not here?"

"Look, Ray," I drew his name out like the sound of a tin can lid squealing open. "I was wondering if you would like to have dinner with me and my kids sometime this week?"

"Is that like a family thing?"

"It sure sounds like a family thing."

"Okay," Ray said. "Okay. I think I'm up for a family thing."

For several years after Dillon was born I hardly worked at all, spending most of my time caring for the two boys. I woke each morning to Dillon crying in his crib. I heated his milk in an enamel saucepan with avocado-colored flowers peeling from the rim. The milk never heated quickly enough to quiet Dillon. My first sensation every morning was the sound of his thirst. The panic of the whole day came to me, exaggerated by my lack of sleep after waiting for Art to come home from his night job as a janitor. Even so, I count most of those days as among the best of my life. They were often long raining days when the boys played in front of the grey windows or summer days so hot and dusty they would sit under the trees in the cool forest among the sword ferns, drinking Cokes and building cities for their green plastic army men.

On one particular morning, I woke and Art lay as he did every morning, but I just slipped my flat-soled canvas shoes on and walked down the dirt driveway while Dillon cried in the boys' room. I walked down the gravel road. Above me the clouds had just started to break up and the trees were black and jagged silhouettes against the rising light. The air held faint wisps of the evening's dampness but I could tell from the brittle clatter of the gravel snapping under the soles of my shoes that the day was going to be hot. At the bottom of our hill, I sat in a strawberry field, way out in the middle of the mounded rows among the green berries and little white flowers and large clods of soil. I looked around me as the sky grew light, just enjoying the morning, and I felt just like myself, not like a mother or a wife.

When I returned home, the door still hung open. Dillon had stopped crying. Milton sat directly in front of our black and white TV eating Cheerios from a round tupperware bowl with a wooden mixing spoon. "Hi, Mom."

He lifted the paddle smoothness of the spoon with a thin coating of milk and Cheerios.

In the bedroom, Art had rolled to one side exposing a single hand, as lifeless as that of a ten-story suicide jumper under a police blanket. I crawled into the bed that was warm and smelled of his musky night odor, and the after-shave scent of his late night drinking. If I had left, I'd be so gone I'd never even have been there in the first place.

I asked Dillon and Milton to set the table and find some chairs before Ray came for dinner. The roast had been in the oven all day and the house smelled warm like roasted onions and garlic and beef. I cut the greens for a salad on the chopping board while Dillon walked back and forth from the kitchen to the main room where we had the long battered table set up. He carried out a stack of earthenware plates and silverware I had bought at a fire sale a couple of weeks before. He carried out a handful of odd-shaped mugs. "Take glasses," I said while I chopped up the red onion. "We only have two, Mom," Dillon said. Finally I checked on the table, and they had forgotten the table cloth, leaving the old peeling-paint surface exposed like the cracked skin of a dry lake bed, and we only had three full-sized chairs. One person would have to sit in one of short grade-school chairs I had bought at the same fire sale.

"It looks nice," I said.

Milton sat in the smallest chair and leaned against the wall. "When does your boyfriend get here?"

"In a while. Why don't you get your tape player and we can listen to some records?"

"I don't want to listen to Crystal Gale," Milton said.

"We can listen to something you like." And that was it. I could hear him running up the stairs.

"What can I do?" Dillon asked.

"You could peel the potatoes."

"Isn't it a little late to be making potatoes?"

"No," I said, "Mr. Ore-Ida, we have about forty minutes before the roast is done, in which time we will have coffee, then salad and wine, and then dinner will be served."

I could hear Milton's music coming out of the other room, deep ringing church bells followed by tinny guitar screeching. Milton slid back into the kitchen and smiled at us. "Hey, hey, Stickbutt, no need to peel the potatoes," he said. "The skins are good for you."

"Good," I said. "I used to not peel them when I was young, *a la hippy*."

"They taste better that way," Milton said.

I pulled the cake out of the refrigerator.

"A cake — " Milton said. "Whose birthday is it? It's not yours. It's not mine. It's not Stickbutt's birthday."

"Don't call Dillon that."

"What should I call him? Roy?"

"Hey," Dillon said. "Roy's a good guy's name."

Milton started to laugh. He sat at the table and laid out the paper napkins. "You crack me up, Stickbutt."

"Boys," I said.

"I could—" Dillon started to say something but Milton stood up and said. "You could what? What?"

"Nothing."

"Come on," I said. "Let's all sit down at the table and have something to eat while we wait for Ray to come."

We sat quietly for a minute listening to Milton's tape.

She was a fast machine. She kept her motor clean,
Was the best damn woman that I ever seen.
She had the sightless eyes telling me no lies
Knocking me out with those American thighs.

"Do you like this?"

"Sure," I said. And then we all started to laugh.

Ray came with a bouquet of tiger lillies, Indian paint brush, and stunted ferns. I grabbed the plants, not sure if we even had a vase. In the kitchen, I lay them on the counter, flung out the dregs from the green plastic juice pitcher. I filled the pitcher with sink water and twirled back into the dining room. It didn't seem like anything had gone wrong yet. I planted the pitcher in the middle of the table. Fluffs of wild cotton weed and spindly strands of grass scattered over the table. Both Dillon and Milton smiled and then laughed when I noticed that Ray had sat in the child sized chair. "Ray, That's my chair."

"What's cooking?"

"Let me at least get you a pillow." I grabbed the pillow from the middle of the living room floor where Dillon watched TV.

I handed Ray the pillow. When he stood up, I swiped the chair away from him and quickly sat.

"Mom," Milton said. "That's Ray's chair. Give it to him."

"She can have her chair," Ray said.

Milton stood up and pulled the chair away from me. "Here you go, Mr. Burke. Mom's just fucking with you. Excuse me, I mean she's just playing with you."

Ray looked at me. "Thanks, I guess. Call me Ray."

"You're welcome, Mr. Burke."

"Call me Ray."

"Sorry, Ray," Milton took a drink of water and looked at me.

"How come you're afraid to say fuck in front of Ray but you have no problem swearing when I'm around?"

"Mom, that's not true," Milton said.

"You don't listen to your mother?" Ray asked. "That is

not a good sign."

"I do listen to her. I'm a very…" Milton looked around the room, searching as fast as he could for the right word, and finally he hit pay dirt: "obedient son."

"Obedient. I would definitely say that's Milton," I said. "Go ahead and dig in."

We ate and Ray kept making moaning noises that made Milton and Dillon laugh. "This is so good." Ray started to ham it up. "Janice," Ray said in a deep, husky voice. "Your cooking is pure ambrosia. Okay. I do. I marry you."

"You can't," Milton said. "You don't even know her."

"Milton, he's just screwing around," I said. "Lighten up."

"Fuck you, Mom."

"Now that seems out of line," Ray lay his fork down. "Don't you think, Milton?"

"No, you don't know my Mom the way I do. She'll just screw with you until you get so mad you don't know what to do. I'm sure she does that to you, Ray."

"I'm Mr. Burke, to you. How can you say something like that to your mother? Didn't your father beat any manners into you?"

We ate in silence then, and I knew that the moment I had worked all afternoon to get to had come and gone. "This is good, Mom," Milton finally said. "But I'm stuffed. Can I be excused?"

"Can I be excused as well?" asked Dillon.

"Sure, you two can leave."

When they had gone upstairs, I started to pack up the leftovers.

"Janice, leave it. The boys or I can pick it all up tomorrow. I want to thank you for inviting me. It was marvelous meal. I brought a bottle of wine but left it in the car. Should I go get it?"

"Get it."

When he came back I asked him, "Why do you treat my kids like that? They're my kids."

"You just don't seem able to defend yourself. Sorry. I was out of line. I'm sure they're not a complete waste. I can sort of see myself in Dillon, when I was his age. I drank a lot of beer. But I didn't go to work as drunk as he did last week. He passed out in the middle of the field. A criminal would go to work that drunk. I'm responsible for this community and I'm not going to let these kids push me around just because I'm dating their mother."

"That really clears your name, doesn't it? 'I'm responsible.' You're the one who dodged the draft. You dropped out of school. They're just kids and they're my kids and you're telling me they're no good. That's bullshit, Ray. You'd treat yourself like shit if you met your twenty-year-old self. Your forty-year-old self would blow your head off."

"I've learned some things. That is all. But I'm basically the same guy I was at nineteen. I listen to the same music. I date the same woman."

"I'm not the same woman."

"What are you talking about? Look at you, brown hair, not a strand of grey, legs like—"

"I dye my hair."

"Two, maybe three wrinkles around your eyes and they're from laughing. You even weigh less."

"I'm fat. Who are you trying to kid?"

"You're even better than young. We're basically the same people."

"Ray, I'm a thirty-seven-year-old woman who spends too much time drinking and smoking dope or thinking about drinking and smoking dope. I have a fifteen-year-old son and a ten-year-old son. And I'm running away from my drug-addicted husband."

"Art's an addict? I thought he smoked dope?"

"He does."

"You can't be addicted to hash. A physical impossibility."

"You're not twenty years old. Neither am I and I don't want to be."

"Sure you do."

"I can't be. I've got two kids upstairs who you treat like shit. What would you do if I treated your kids like you treat them?"

"They're punks, Janice. Get rid of them. Live with me."

"How would I get rid of them?"

"I can take care of them."

"You will?"

"I can have my foreman drive them out to one of the logging roads. It'll solve all your problems."

"Like a litter of cats I don't want?"

"Exactly, just like a litter of cats you don't need. And then we can be like we wanted to be when we were twenty in Seattle. I'll read you poetry while you sit in my work shirt by the stove drinking hot chocolate."

"You are a sick man," I said. "But you don't even know how tempting that is." I leaned over the table, grabbed the neck of the wine bottle and poured myself another glass. "Really, you don't mind the boys. Because it looks like you're going to kill them."

"They need that."

"I don't think so. They've already had that and it hasn't done any good."

"I can handle them."

"Ray," I said. "There's been something else bothering me."

"You've been thinking a lot."

"Tell me about the woman who lived here."

"We dated for a long time," Ray said. "Years. She

wouldn't marry me but she talked me into letting her move into this house. Did we bring that bottle of wine up here?"

"Are you trying to change the subject?"

"I could use a glass, is all."

"Did you like her?" I asked.

"I loved her but she was really moody. I just assumed that all women were moody. But it turned out she was crazy. Really. It wasn't the kind of thing I noticed. She started to swing, one week giddy, one week under the weather, one week bouncing off the walls, next week she won't get out of bed. She wouldn't let me come over sometimes. She demanded that Marigold Greer come out, but not me. So I told Mrs. Greer she couldn't come over. She came anyway because Amanda had told Mrs. Greer that she had been her mother in a past life. And I guess Mrs. Greer believed her or wanted to believe, or whatever. Amanda also told Mrs. Greer that I beat her, all kinds of stuff. I should have taken her to the hospital, but I was afraid of losing her. You know how it is in the movies. They always cut out the best part of a person in those hospitals. And sometimes being with Amanda was better than I could imagine and I wouldn't change that. I'd come out here and she'd have a bucket full of ice and cold tea out in the field with a starched linen sheet for shade and she'd sing old songs she'd learned from her father in Rock Springs. And it was something I felt I couldn't risk losing. I mean the bad times didn't seem that bad on days like those. And then they found her floating in the Laughing Horse. Almost eight years ago now. Then John's family moved in. I suppose a lot of people have been here over the years."

I lay my head on his chest. He held me for the longest time. Finally, I led him upstairs, and I slowly took his clothes off, but I didn't feel like messing around, or maybe he wasn't able to have sex in this house now. It felt like I was her, Amanda, doing it to him. "I'm sort of creeped out," I told him.

"It's okay," he said. He held me and I fell asleep. His body felt cool and solid next to me. I took a breath and another breath and then for a long space of time I didn't hear a thing from him and finally he took a breath. And the whole bit started over again. He held me next to him, and I knew if I stayed with Ray that was how it would be. He would hold me so that he knew he was with someone who understood where he had come from, not because he really wanted me there. Anyone who found herself in Bainesville at his door, whom he had known all those years past, could have been in this spot. I wondered how this woman had felt with him. I wondered if, when she spoke, Ray listened to her.

In the morning I woke when he slid out of bed, letting the covers slide off my legs, exposing them to the cold air. It felt good on my knees and I thought for a second about getting out of bed and making coffee for Ray, but then I pulled the covers back on. "Why do you have to go? Stay in bed with me." I watched him standing in the early morning sunlight. Though the room was bright with it and Ray stood in a patch of light, his typing-paper-white feet on the wood floor, covered in sunlight, I could see his breath and the way his skin constricted and goosebumped on his chest

"I have a ranch to run," he said.

"Stay. If you were twenty, you'd stay."

"Not if I had to work."

"I remember a time when you didn't even call in sick to stay in bed with me. You just never went back to work."

"Well, I can't do that now. I'll be back, okay?" Ray tucked his shirt in and crawled onto the blankets. He rolled them around me, tucked them under me and brought his morn-ing-beard-sharp face up against my cheek. He kissed me and then left. As soon as I heard his truck go down the driveway, I slipped out of bed, suddenly confused about everything. I didn't shower or anything. I found my night-gown bunched on the floor.

I rinsed the butcher knife in the kitchen sink, and went up into the attic. Faint morning light came through the round window in the far wall. I ran my finger around the cabinet, and then edged the knife blade in until I had could insert the metal between the frame and the door. Then I slid it into the wall and popped the cabinet open. For a second I could see only the black cavity of the cabinet's interior and then I made out a shoe box that had started to come apart. Balls of paper had sloughed from the edges. A box camera sat on its side, covered in a film of webs and dust. I opened the card board box and found hundreds of photographs whose faces and expres-sions were meaningless to me, except they all had the same sloping forehead and the same Sunday smile. The faces all looked like variations of Mrs. Greer. From the sharp, hard handwriting on the back, I could see that several of the photographs were even older than this house. I had always wondered if my mother kept a box like this some-where, the old family photos; somehow I didn't think they existed. We had moved too much, and we had lost all con-tact with her family. I closed the door, leaving the photos as they were because Marigold Greer at least knew they were here.

I wanted to get of the house. Downstairs I put on my tennis shoes and jacket and I went outside and started walking into the forest. Under the trees, the sunlight hadn't come yet and it seemed like evening. Turning around in the meadow, I looked up into the tops of the trees; they rose up into the sky like long fingers keeping the dark shadow-night next to the ground. I ran through the forest.

Halfway up the hill, I took off my shoes and ran like Marigold Greer said Amanda had run. I felt the sudden intensity of each step because the ground held the crinkled edges of the Oregon Grape and the dry mat of pine needles, and then the damp, grainy soil under them. Suddenly this mundane and obvious chore of running through the forest became an ordeal as the distance between where I was and where I had left my shoes expanded. I finally arrived at the top of the ridge, my feet throbbing and cut. I came out of the woods to the marshy edge of the Laughing Horse Reservoir in the morning sunlight. I turned to look down the steep slope to the valley where our house sat and then back to the mountains above the water. And I knew what I wanted; I couldn't live here anymore. I knew I would leave the house. Too many things had happened there and plenty more things were going to happen there.

An American home is a raw place with ghosts so new that the flesh hasn't even rotted off their buried skeletons. I couldn't take being alone in a place with any history. I'd be alone as soon as Ray drove my kids away. My kids would toughen but I didn't want them to get too tough. I'd at least have my kids without Ray. Kids don't have any history. Blank slates, right? Except all the nicks and scars they get from people handling them.

Jolly Rancher

———— • ————

She came into my room to kiss me goodbye. I hadn't actually thought about Mom really going away to my grandmother's funeral, until I smelled the sharp odor of Camel cigarettes and the faint vapor of Green Apple hard candy as she leaned down and kissed me on my upper cheek, right next to my ear lobe. "Good bye, honey," Mom said. She kept Jolly Ranchers in a glass bowl on the kitchen counter because she was on a diet and didn't really like them. On her day off, she always lay on the sofa in her bathrobe until late in the afternoon, reading, painting her nails, and chewing on the candies. She meticulously rolled the wrappers into little balls and stuffed them into her pockets.

When I woke, Mom was completely gone. Looking into her bedroom, the sheets tossed on her bed, her limp and empty Ed's # 1 Diner uniform hanging in the corner, I became worried that she wouldn't ever come back after she went to Grandma's funeral. She might inherit so much money that she could do anything. I walked in tight circles around the kitchen floor. I brushed the counter with my hands and listened to the voices in the courtyard outside the window. I missed my mother's presence in the kitchen as she looked up from her cup of coffee and magazine and smiled at me while I poured my cereal into my specially carved wooden bowl my older brother Milton had made for me in Shop.

A note written with a purple permanent marker, smelling like glue and grapes, read, "Son, wash dishes and vacuum. I left some money for groceries. Love." On the refrigerator door, under a flat Sesame Street Grover magnet, a creased five dollar bill filled a white business envelope. I ate a piece of toast and drank a glass of milk while sitting on the couch. This morning, I had to get to work.

I worked as lawn help at Happy Kids Happy Place Daycare. I found the job a week before the last day of the eighth grade. I worked for the owner's daughter, an older girl named Pam who had just graduated from high school. One time, when I had spent hours removing the grass turf along the sidewalk and breaking the clods into dirt and roots, Pam suddenly kissed me on the lips, bringing her face to mine at a right angle and firmly pressing her lips into mine. She kept her face close to mine, as if she would kiss me again. "You're such a hard worker," she said. Then she turned around, shook her hair, and ran inside. I stood in the yard and rubbed my lips. I wondered if I could count it as a first kiss because it had happened so quickly and I didn't know for sure if she meant anything by it. People do stuff all the time that they don't mean. When my brother Milton still lived with us, I cleaned up after him all the time and whenever Milton was in the same room my mother would tell me that I was a hard worker.

As I left and went down the dark stairs of the apartment building, a black figure blocked the narrow passageway. "Where's your mother?"

"She's in Spokane."

In the partial light, I saw the wrinkled bump in Ms. Krantz the manager's nose, and I smelled the air from her apartment, fried tortilla shells and damp, frayed Persian rugs. "She's coming back?" she asked in a flat voice full of the static of loose phlegm.

"Yeah, I think so."

"Tell her to come see me before she even gets through the door." Ms. Krantz drifted into the light. I hurried behind her, past the swimming pool in the middle of the central courtyard, and out the front gate.

Even though the front door of the daycare had a doorbell, I knocked because Pam didn't want me waking the sleeping children. Pam cracked the door, letting out the hubbub of a laughing baby. Brushing a strand of hair out of her face, she smiled at me. "I'm sorry about your grandmother." She closed the door behind her, letting it rest on its hinge. She wore a pair of tight shorts that I liked to see her wear. We walked along the row of rhododendrons, over the cropped grass of the back play yard to the work shed. "Is your Mom going to inherit a lot of money? Will we have to find a new yard boy?"

"I'm not a yard boy," I said. "I'm the yard man."

"Don't get me started," Pam said. "Is your Mom out of town this weekend?"

"Why?"

"She is, isn't she?" We stood in the shed. It smelled of motor oil, gasoline, and lawn clippings. Pam read the list of my jobs from a legal pad. When she finished reading, she said, "Everything understood?" I nodded and Pam rattled the pad onto its hook, next to the lawn rake. "You know my friend Molly?" Molly went to the high school where Pam had just graduated. Sometimes Molly sunbathed on the back lawn while she waited for Pam to finish her work. Molly never wore make-up. Her skin was pale and she had blotches around her mouth, but because she was older and once had a boyfriend, I thought she was sexy.

"She likes you," Pam said.

"How? She does?"

"She thinks you have a cute butt."

"You're making fun of me."

"You like her?"

"I need to start work," I said. I grabbed the lawn mower's handle and shoved it toward the door.

"She's coming over today."

"I'll be at home packing so when my Mom comes with my grandmother's million dollars, I'll be ready."

"Today, in reality," Pam said. "Molly said she'd like to come over to your house and visit you."

"I don't know."

"I told her you'd love it, so think about it while you finish your work," Pam said and I thought about it. I thought about Molly and her skinny arms and her long fingers and the way her hair fell in rolling curls down her back. When she came over, she usually wore a one-piece swimsuit under a pair of old jeans. I wondered why she wanted to visit me. I had never really talked to Molly, although every time she came over she nodded her head at me and I smiled and turned away because I didn't want her to know that I sometimes thought about the way she kept her purse close to her, and would sometimes open it up to take out a small silver mirror and look into her own eyes. After mowing, I spent the morning weeding the flower beds and tossing the weeds into a small bucket that I dumped in the compost heap in the back. After my four hours, I told Pam I was leaving. "So did you think about it?" she asked.

"She can come over if she wants."

"She said she would be at your house around three."

"Three?" I asked. Once I was on the road, I ran home, closed the screen door behind me, and climbed the steps to the apartment. The hard odor of fried eggs filled the passage. On the door to my apartment, the brass number six had fallen, leaving a raised ridge of paint running around the old outline. Under the six, the eye-lens had popped out, and my mother had jammed a cigarette butt into the peep hole. Both things had happened late one night when my father, Mom's ex-husband, had tried to beat the door down and get into the apartment. I had looked for the eye lens. For a while I took out the cigarette butts, but Mom would stuff in another one. She told me to leave it alone because people walking down the hallway would see the hole and then they would look in and God knows what they'd see. Eventually I didn't see the filled hole; it blended with the door's flaking paint and scuffs.

I looked from the kitchen window onto the apartment courtyard. Sometimes, women lay almost naked on the lawn chairs next to the pool. But now, the wooden lounge chairs held their empty arms into the air. The apartment building was quiet. My mother normally sat on the sofa, watching TV, painting her toenails, getting ready for work, but now she was gone.

Sweating from the run home, covered with cinders of chewed grass, I vacuumed the living room, vacuumed my mother's bedroom, and wiped the kitchen clean. I tried to imagine what Molly would do when she stepped into the apartment. But I didn't know. She could step through the door and throw off her clothes right there. She might arrive wearing a dress that I would try to unzip, but the zipper would get stuck and she'd leave because I was so stupid. I wondered what she would wear. I hoped she didn't wear a bra because guys in the movies always had a hard time taking them off.

I stopped in the middle of the living room, suddenly spazzing. My intestines fought for room with my stomach. My back itched in all of the places I couldn't reach. I tore off my shoes so that I could scratch the soles of my feet, but sitting Indian style on the carpet, I dug my nails into the hard skin until the soles of my feet were bright red and still I couldn't get rid of the itching. So I took a shower turned as hot as I could turn the dial, until the round edges of my shoulders burned.

As I showered, I thought about my mother driving all the way back to Ephrata, way out in the desert on the other side of the mountains, and I started to calm down. I remembered what the road looked like from the front seat of the old car we used to have, a Supersport Impala convertible. When my older brother wasn't hogging the front seat, I'd sit there and just look at the yellow line coming toward us. I'd try to spot the furthest one from the car and just watch it come down the road toward us. But almost every time, it'd zip toward the hood so fast I had no chance of seeing it. I never really knew my grandmother, but I don't think she had a dime. I didn't really think my mother would just disappear. Sometimes, Mom did leave for a long time, but in the end, she always came back.

Dry, and wearing a pair of nylon jogging shorts and a yellow T-shirt, I ate Saltine crackers, American cheese, and an apple. While I ate, I looked at the *TV Guide*. I occasionally paused to look out the window of the apartment. I broke a slice of cheese into two rectangles and then again into four squares. I put each square on a single saltine and put it into my mouth. Outside, brackish water filled the pool basin and a woman now lay in one of the wooden lawn chairs on the patio. The lit panel of a Coke machine glittered in the shadows. The woman spread her towel over the chair, leaned over her black plastic radio, turned a knob and lay back to rub oil over her arms and legs until the sun reflected from her skin. I could see she had already tanned an even brown.

From the change jar in my room, I found two quarters. I walked into the courtyard. The woman lay with her face pressed into the chair. I walked in the shadow of the overhang. Gently, I pushed on the glowing Coke panel, a can dropped from the machine. She looked at me. I couldn't see her eyes behind her sun glasses, but her head tilted and rose along my body. As I walked close to her, by the pool of water that smelled like moldy bread, I saw that her arms were very thin and her legs were extremely skinny except at the place her legs joined her body. The round heap of her soft butt and her fleshy back seemed oddly overstuffed. Her hair clumped in a knot bunched at the back of her head. "Hi," she said without lifting her head from the chair.

"Hi," I croaked and I stepped into the shadows of the hallway. From the kitchen window, I saw she had turned over, exposing a tan line along the top of her breasts. I dropped the Coke in the refrigerator. I pulled out my box with the *Green Lantern* and *Justice League* comic books. Among the giant-sized issues of the *Green Lantern,* I stored a *Penthouse* I had found while cleaning the dumpster behind the daycare. In one pictorial, the naked woman lay next to a swimming pool, pushing her body into the water and into the furniture around the pool. I pictured the woman outside as the woman inside the photographs. Instead of "Hi," she said, "I can't quite get this oil on a couple of spots on my back." After I finished, I checked the room to see if it looked the same as it did before. I hid the magazine in its place.

Molly knocked on the door at two forty and I ran to the door and swung it open. She stepped back and asked me, "Does Dillon live here?" She recognized me and smiled, "Oh, hi." She wore a green sweat shirt, jeans and a pair of earrings that twirled just above her shoulders. She wore fresh lipstick that made her look like she had put on wax lips. She and I looked at each other for a moment without saying anything. She glanced up and down the hall.

"Come on in," I said.

"Nice place." She threw her bag down on the sofa, and walked through the kitchen. "Jolly Ranchers, my favorite. Can I have some?"

"Sure," I said, "We have a thousand."

She unwrapped a Mandarin Flavor, and rolled the hard candy into her cheek. "What's down there?" she asked. She pointed toward the bedrooms. I followed her. She put her hand on her pocket and leaned into Mom's bedroom.

"You shouldn't go in there," I said. "My room's right here… "

"Yeah," she said. She flipped on the light to my mother's bedroom. Her bed was unmade and a suitcase with peeling leather buckles sat open on the crumpled sheets with a few folded blouses in it. Next to the bed sat a small glass end table with an old clock that had numbers that snapped into place every time the minutes changed. The clock made a buzzing noise.

"We shouldn't go in here," I said. But Molly opened the top drawer to the dresser.

"Hubba hubba," Molly said. She pulled out a slinky slip

and a lacy square of fabric. She pulled it open and I saw that it was some sort of body suit. "Someone around here has some taste," she said.

"What do we have here?" she said. She held up a small carved box. She opened it and said, "Goldmine!"

"Don't take anything," I said. I grabbed the box out of Molly's hands. The contents fell out. A baggie opened as it fell to the carpet and scattered leaves and seeds over the floor.

"Look what you did," Molly said. "Get a broom."

I came back and we swept up the marijuana as best as we could. As soon as we had it all back in the baggie, Molly said, "Let's smoke some."

"Is that why you came over?"

"Come on, just a little."

"I don't smoke it," I said. "My Dad smoked it. My Mom says she doesn't smoke it."

"Then she won't miss it, will she?"

"No," I said.

Molly sat back and said, "I'll make it worth your while."

I looked at her. She held the body suit in her lap, stroking the fabric. "You have to promise that we won't take very much," I said.

"Promise," she said. She measured a little out into the wrinkle of her palm. "Do you have a can?"

"I've got a Coke, but I haven't drunk it yet."

"Let's go drink it," Molly said.

Molly poured the Coke into a glass and then pushed the can down in the middle. She took a corn cob holder and poked a bunch of holes in the hollow she had pushed into the can. With a lighter from her purse, she lit the leaves and seeds. Smoke rolled out of the lip of the can. I thought she was an expert. I had never seen anyone use a can before. My father used a pipe or rolled the weed up into papers.

"Suck it in," Molly said, holding her breath. I held the can and drew the smoke in. The can made a wheezing noise and I tasted the Coca-Cola, and then I tasted a familiar hiss of smoke as it hit my throat. It felt dry and I sucked in more smoke. I grunted the way my father always did. The ashes in the hollow of the can turned red. Molly grabbed the can back and sucked in more smoke.

"That's it," she said.

I let out my breath. Smoke poured from my nose and my mouth. A pool of blue smoke drifted across the kitchen. Molly smiled at me. Finally she let out her smoke. "This is good shit," she said. She shook her head.

I thought she was just pretending.

Molly took my hand and we stood up and went into the living room. We sat on the sofa and she didn't look at me, but smiled straight ahead. She dug around in her purse and then unwrapped something that she put into her mouth.

She scooted close to me and I scooted close to her so we both sat in the middle of the couch and then she placed her hands on my face. I leaned back. Then she pushed me back into the couch so that I was laying down. Her hair exploded over my face, and I felt the slightly damp warmth of her tongue on my neck and I smelled the cinnamon odor of a red gummy bear. "Are you eating candy?" I asked. I wondered if this could be counted as my first kiss? Already, it was gone and I was more concerned with the unexpected taste in her mouth.

"Yeah. Jolly Rancher. Fire Flavor. Want some?"

"Yes," I said.

"I wish Jolly Rancher made a condom because then I'd have both of my favorite things in one package." Molly sat back on the couch and told me that I should take off my clothes if I wanted a Jolly Rancher.

"You first," I said.

Molly stripped off her shirt. She wore a loose white tank top without a bra. "That's cheating," I said. "You still have a top on."

She took off her tank top.

I stared at her nipples. They didn't look like anything that I had expected. They didn't end like little buttons at the tips of her breasts but sort of spread out into her skin. I couldn't tell where they started or ended. "You didn't have to," I started to say, but she turned to her bag and pulled out a handful of Jolly Ranchers. She gave me a red one and popped a green one in her mouth, and then pressed me to the couch.

"You need to take off your clothes." She breathed heavily into my ear. She started sucking on my mouth and the wedge of Green Apple popped out of her mouth and slid into my mouth.

"Hey," I said. But then I found my shirt around my head and felt my pants loosen around my waist. "Hey, hey, hey," I said.

"Hey, hey," she said.

But nothing would happen for me. Molly laboured until three-thirty when I gave up and said, "It was great, but I can't go on." I knew I shouldn't have looked at my magazine today.

"But you didn't come," Molly said. Our clothes lay around the couch and two sticky Jolly Ranchers had fallen between the cushions.

"Shall I make you some lunch?" I asked.

"Sure. What've you got?"

"American cheese."

"Creamy."

"Saltine crackers?"

"No, that's too dry."

"Peanut butter and jelly sandwiches?"

"Perfect," Molly said. She put on her clothes and sat in the kitchen watching me make the sandwiches.

"You like your bread toasted?" I asked.

"So how was it, considering?"

"Good. Fine. Bread cut diagonally or horizontally?"

"No cutting," Molly said. "Just good? First time's usually the best."

"Not according to my Mom," I said. "She said the first time was the worst in the world. And then she said that it got better. She said you've got to practice."

"You mean I wasn't good?"

"I don't know. It was my first time. Right now it was the best."

"Yeah, I thought it was nice."

"It was also the worst, being the first time because I've got nothing else to compare it to." I sat at the table with Molly and put her plate in front of her.

"I'm not hungry now."

"I'm starving," I said. "Don't you want your sandwich?"

"You can have it," she said. She opened the door with the brass number six. "Thanks for the bud," she said. Then she slammed the door shut behind her. I left her sandwich on the table. I cleaned up the couch and looked for anything that I could find that would tip off my mother that a girl beside her had been in the house. I found the two sticky bits of candy behind the sofa. I felt an odd, lightheaded feeling, like I had forgotten to eat.

At nine o'clock the next morning I woke to the sound of the garbage truck coming down the street, crashing dumpsters. Cool air leaked from the window and the smell of the pool, harsh, rotting, and vegetable, jolted me awake. I showered and hurried down the steps to work.

At the daycare, Pam opened the door.

"So how was it with Molly? Did you and her have a good time?"

"Sure."

"Sure? You're very gallant about it."

"What are you doing this afternoon?"

"Not much."

"My Mom'll still be in Eastern Washington. Would you like to come over?"

"Would you fix me a peanut butter and jelly sandwich?" She laughed but it was a sound that didn't make me laugh with her. I wondered where that left my first kiss.

That evening, I saw my mother's car pull slowly into her parking spot. Ms. Krantz followed her up into the apartment. I heard the landlady's bray over my mother's laugh. They sat on the sofa. "Hi, honey, Ms. Krantz is having an important conversation with me. Give me ten minutes."

I sat on my bed in my room. Blankets lumped around my back and across my thighs. I heard the muffled voices of my mother and the landlady talking softly. I remembered my mother had called Ms. Krantz a bitch and a whore when Ms. Krantz had picked up the trash outside, when Mom had sat at the front window, reading the classified section of the *Times*. When she had seen Ms. Krantz's waddling figure, Mom swallowed her coffee and spit out the words under her breath.

I listened to their voices in the other room. "Your mother must have left you something. Everyone has a little something when they die," Ms. Krantz said. "I've held off giving you and your son notice because I expected you to return with rent."

"I don't have it."

I heard Ms. Krantz cough. "Well, that is all I need to know at the moment. Remember about your visitor as well."

She was talking about my father. She always called him that.

"If I see that man around here again, I'll call the cops. That man who's been selling you whatever it is you're taking will be caught. I don't want those kind of folks clogging up my hallways anymore. So if you got to have them people around here, you had better move."

Mom's hair fell back from her temples, and rolled around her ears. In the daylight, Mom's face, her jaw and her nose, broke into thousands of incongruous lines, scribbling along the arc of her cheekbone. I saw a terrain of stray hairs, peach fuzz, moles, and blackheads. I wanted to feel my mother's presence then as a source of immediate comfort and safety, a place where I could ask for money or go to feel the warmth of her arms and the bulk of her body wrap around me. I was a little taller than her now and I don't think she was used to it because she stumbled back as I stepped toward her. "Sit down," she said. I sat on the sofa, and she sat next to me. She brushed her skirt, and a Jolly Rancher wrapper flicked onto the carpet. Tossing back her hair, she tapped the end of a cigarette on the back of her right hand palm, and then propped it into her mouth while she hugged me. "I missed you. Did you miss me?"

When I said yes, she smiled and put out her cigarette and lit another one, but I felt odd now wrapped in her arms. She blew smoke out the window and blew some at the pane of glass. I smelled her hair. A cache of familiar smoke held me strongly against her.

Sewage Lagoon

———•———

I couldn't go back to my apartment because the woman I live with had told me that if I ever came home drunk she wouldn't even say anything; she would just drive down the block to the U-Haul franchise behind the Big-O Tires, and come back with whatever truck they had waiting for her, and take everything, even the oak rocking chair where I always sat by the window on Sundays reading *The Rise and Fall of the Roman Empire*. This one would do it, too. It was her chair.

Marjorie's favorite trick: She asks me to go the grocery store with a particular list of things like bay leaves, muffin pan liners, linseed oil among the usual eggs, cheese, milk and hamburger, and when I forget this or that she asks, "and what did you get?" She pulls out the receipt and audits the money in my wallet. "You had twenty-six dollars in your billfold. The receipt is for twelve-fifty." She actually said this one time. "You're missing about four bucks." She constantly assessed things. Bottom line, she had to be ready to leave at any moment because she knew I was an alcoholic, albeit an undrinking one. Alcohol remained the defining non-act of my life. Instead of being the drunk who dropped by the mini-mart on the way home to buy two forty ouncers of Mad Dog, I had become the former drunk who couldn't risk dropping by the mini-mart even to buy a bag of Lay's Sour Cream and Onion potato chips.

Marjorie met her first husband at A.A. "Yes, I used to drink," Marjorie's A.A. spiel ran. "Although that's misleading because drink implies that I would eventually stop to swallow and breathe. Since my lungs could process gasoline, and since my throat was in a constant state of swallowing, I essentially had a bottle for a mouth. I didn't even want air between me and my booze." When she told me this the first time, I had to hand it to her. She had been there. Marjorie reconditioned her first husband, helped him get God, and a job, and then he traded her in for a woman who could have kids. "The ground rules are simple. If you even smell like after-shave I will leave you." She had learned with her ex-husband to never drop the poise, to never settle back in her chair and stay awhile, to never forget what it was like to be an alcoholic. She always watched me, she said, because she watched herself. And that was exactly what I thought I wanted.

One day after work, I opened my wallet and thought I was missing five bucks. My immediate response wasn't who stole this five dollars, or even that Marjorie would really get pissed if I couldn't account for the five dollars, but I wondered if I had bought a beer and didn't remember drinking it. On the drive back to Marjorie's apartment, I retraced my steps, trying to account for each step in my day, but before I could account for that five dollars I said, screw this, and drove straight to my old place and ordered a round of Budweiser.

My old place, in the days before Marjorie, was Jackie's Inn, a tavern at the edge of Everett's old lumber yards and docks. The bar itself had been outfitted in tavern memorabilia from the fifties. A Miller shade hung over the pool table, an out-of-place plastic imitation of Victorian parlor glass. A rubber woman, in denim shorts and a shirt tightly encasing her thick thighs and breasts levered the caps off beer bottles with her serrated tin teeth. A long Coors Silver Bullet mirror lined the space behind the bar. The tables were thick, solid wood and slung low to the faded linoleum. A popcorn machine ticked on the counter. A hot dog roaster rolled oily frankfurters. The only other patron in the bar nodded his head when I ordered the beer. "Obliged," he said, and turned back to the sputtering TV quickly enough to let me know he wouldn't be buying me any drinks.

The old crowd had obviously dried out. When I rattled off my list of where's so and so, the woman who ran the place—all I can remember about this woman was that her name wasn't Jackie—shook her head, "I don't know. Stopped coming by a long time ago." I listened to the Stones on the compact disk jukebox and read some more of Gibbons. I drank and looked out the window at the nearly empty street. Minutes passed before a car drove slowly past the line of hotels and hardware supply stores that filled this part of Everett. Drinking beer after beer, I knew I didn't have to do any accounting; I knew where the money was going. At two o'clock, the woman who wasn't Jackie said, "Bar's closed." She locked the door behind me and the other guy. He slowly made his way down the sidewalk and I stumbled into the driver's seat of the Subaru Brat and swerved to my favorite park to sleep and hopefully wake up rational enough to decide what I wanted to do.

Marjorie had made it clear what she would do. I had six years on her and already she seemed older than me.

She wore her hair in a sensible bob sprinkled with gray hairs. She sat up in bed from eight-thirty to nine-fifteen reading S.S. Van Dine, J.A. Jance, K.K. Beck, civilized murder mysteries. When she turned off her light, she fell promptly to sleep. We were both readers, but her books seemed so sensible. They were short and cheap. She bought them second-hand for the price of a pack of cigarettes. She wasn't pretentious enough to call them literature, but she did learn things from them, little tidbits about the way fortune tellers scam customers, nothing useful, but interesting stuff. They must've been funny, because she always chuckled while she read them. Marjorie also liked to walk.

The next morning I woke in my favorite place in Everett, the natural preserve along the reclaimed industrial tidal flats where Interstate 5 comes north out of town. The black odor of river mud and rotting milkweed and brine soaked through the Brat and drove out the reek of unfiltered Camels and alcohol-induced sweat. The weight of all the time I'd wasted, the family I'd lost, and how close I was to losing even this woman who at least understood me pressed a flood of thoughts out of me, thoughts I didn't really want to have at six o' clock in the morning. Even last summer, when Marjorie introduced me to this place, seemed like years and years ago. We came here to walk along the river slough to the site of an old farm. Between the freeway and the smooth surface of the lake, a sewage treatment plant's huge rotor spiraled water up into filter tanks, like a massive toy, a gizmo with seemingly useless moving parts.

My son, Dillon, had once left a plastic truck in my over-grown lawn. The grass had curled up during the months since my last dry spell. I had woke restless one morning and had started to mow the front yard. The Evinrude mower had mixed Dillon's Mac truck into shards of yellow plastic and mulched grass. The blades had flung a hanger-wire thin axle into my thigh. I hadn't noticed it at first. I had felt a prick on the back of my leg. I had reached back to scratch the itch and had felt an inch of wire jutting from under my butt cheek. I touched a nub sticking out under my front jeans pocket. Blood hadn't even started to flow yet. I hadn't known who to blame, my son for having hid the truck in the lawn, or myself for not being home enough to mow the place. Later, I still walked with a limp when I went to prison and it had become known I had been wounded in a knife fight.

Blackberries had grown along the Snohomish River in huge clumps. With Marjorie asking me not to go into the bushes, I had stepped into them and filled my Seahawk's cap with the rich fruit and ate as I walked along with her. The heavy berries had tasted a little rancid, almost artificial, like they had been molded from Crisco. I had gorged on them. Past the tidal flats and the old farm, near the lake, the bushes had grown mountainous. The swollen vines looked like purple garden hoses. I had filled cap after cap with the berries and ate and ate until I passed a fence with a sign that read, "Do Not Enter. Sewage Lagoon." I realized then what I had thought was a wide, natural lake, was a shallow pond of raw sewage fermenting in the treatment process. Every toilet bowl, every sewer pipe, really everything, emptied into this artificial lake that surrounded the North Everett Sewage Treatment Plant. These flat ponds were filled with algae and birds swept out of the sky and landed on the smooth water, shattering the reflection of the Three Sisters and Mount Rainier.

Before I met Marjorie and especially before I met the girl before her, I can tell you, I was feeling worthless and like I had lived my entire life. I had wasted the years I lived with my first wife, Janice, smoking pot and just floating through the long evenings listening to records until I was busted the first time. I didn't even notice my children growing up under me. In the King County Jail, I was turned onto coke, and I started a higher profile business in the boom eighties, until I was finally busted again. I'd just finished two years at the Washington State Correctional Facility in Monroe, and I didn't know where Janice or my two kids had gone. Where do you start looking for people you figure don't want to be found anyway?

I started working lunch making fish and chips and hamburgers in Everett where my parole officer worked. For the first couple of months, I spent most evenings at the library. I had become used to an iron-clad schedule in prison. Once you find a routine, it's hard to change.

Everett was an old Navy town held hostage by people that didn't even know they had the place by the balls. This sounds like a joke, but it's not: what's the difference between a couple of years active military duty and a couple of years time? The food's the same. You sleep in a bunk in a room with other men who've had their heads shaved. You don't control time. I think the difference between a soldier and a convict is that rules force a soldier to kill for money while most of the folks languishing in prison got there because they broke the rules in order to get money, or they killed someone free of charge.

Jason Blume, my cellmate, was eighteen when he shot his father and mother and little brothers in a farmhouse just outside Carnation, on the Snoqualmie River. He and I talked a lot because we know the same places along the river and, unlike most of the people filling that prison, we had grown up along the banks of the Snoqualmie and Snohomish Rivers and knew where Monroe was in the scheme of the world. These out-of-state drug dealers who'd set up residence in the Seattle neighborhoods of Lynnwood or Ballard or Capitol Hill suddenly found themselves out in the woods, out in the middle of fucking no where, where I suppose they believed a prison should be. The killer, Jason Blume, and I knew the hills around the prison. We talked about what it would be like to escape into the Cascade Mountains where we would live a life of plenty and isolation in the steep valleys and live like Emerson. For me it had always been a fantasy. I had always thought I could make it out there. Jason Blume cupped his coffee, and sat back in the chair. He looked out the high windows at the surrounding hills and mountains, scowling so hard his lips buckled. The light from the window caught on the hard rims of his brown irises. "I could fucking do it, man. I've been out there before. For weeks and weeks my brothers and I would just hike along the ridge tops. When we were hungry we would slip down and fish a lake, pick blueberries, and feast like wild men." He sat in our cell, nostalgic and a little manic about his family who he'd tied down in the vinyl kitchen chairs and executed.

So I guess prison was like a mind-opening experience for me. I made new friends with the kind of people I would never have made friends with before. I realized that if someone like Jason Blume could come to terms with what he'd done, even to the point of missing his victims, I had a lot to look forward to. It wasn't like I'd killed anybody. Afterwards, they returned me to the only town in the Pacific Northwest that made sense for a man just out of prison, Everett, with its wide well-neoned boulevards. Navy hot shits zipped up and down Everett streets in new

Nissans and Mazdas. Old boys from way up river or from the salmon fishing fleet, out for a night of drinking and whoring, hollered to each other on the street corners.

I was rehabilitated and they threw me into a place like that.

I had been going to the library for a couple of months and just enjoying the smallest things, like being able to walk down the pier and sitting in the damp winter night smoking Camel after Camel. I started to drink. At least, I figured, it wasn't illegal. Soon I drank so much, it ought to have been illegal. I had a string of places I liked to go, ending every night around two o'clock with the same crowd of tired faces at Jackie's Inn. By mid-pay check I'd be so poor I'd have to survive on Red Rose Wine and food from the grill where I worked. Sitting in the library, reading a Louis L'Amour, when I was aching from not even being able to drink, I realized I hadn't made it. I looked out the window, not even able to concentrate on this high flying Western, and I wanted to get high because it was better than this. I could sell and snort and just roll along faster and faster until something gave. I knew I needed to start something. I picked up a course catalog for the local community college on the way back to my apartment. At home I circled two classes and on payday I immediately cashed my check and enrolled in two classes.

The night before the first day of school, I was so nervous that I ironed my second-hand oxford shirt and dug out a tie I had once bought for interviewing years before when my ex-wife Janice and I had still been dating. How this particular thing, this tie, had lasted for all of these years, when so many things, not even sofas and houses had survived, made me chuckle at how stupid things can turn out. I'd take the houses back, sure, but it was sort of nice to have this tie to wear on the first day of school. I thought I looked sharp. The tie had been made so long ago that it was beyond style. It had that early sixties look, splattered lines of color falling away to a deep blue background.

I fell asleep remembering college, the rallies, the girls with long hair who would go to class stoned out of their skulls, and the long afternoons attempting to study in the library but instead talking to the kids around me and eventually heading off to their places to drink wine and listen to records. I mean, sure, school had probably changed, but if I was to make a comparison with how everything else had changed, I'm sure kids weren't just drinking beer and smoking dope anymore. I was worried I wouldn't be able to keep up.

The kids in my first class were younger than my own children were now. They didn't talk to each other. They all had short hair, backpacks, and stacks of books. They silently took notes during lecture and hurried out of the room, quickly withdrawing from the minimalist Quonset hut-style buildings, leaving them as flat as helium balloons four days after the party. In all that rush amid the kiosks announcing lectures and concerts and film series, I felt like I was in the middle of things, not exactly someone involved in it, but more like the principal sitting in on the class of a young teacher.

One day, after class, Marjorie, one of the kids my age, fell in next to me as I left my archeology class. "You're new," she said. "Getting your associate's?"

"I don't know. Maybe." I stopped and she stood next to me. She wore a faded sweat shirt and blue jeans, but I could tell she was thin under the bulk of her clothes. Her hair had been pulled back in a barrette, an oversized silver clasp. Her hair, a scraggly blonde color fading to gray at the edges was natural and something I sort of liked. She didn't pretend that she was one of the kids. She seemed sort of settled into her middle-aged body like a person settled into a chair for a long read with a difficult book.

"Name's Marjorie," she said. And then she walked away.

I kept my eye on her. And I could tell she watched me. If I had known any of her friends, I would have written her a note.

I started to sometimes drink coffee with Marjorie and a few of her cronies, older student like me who had already lived lives in the outside world. We valued the community college promise of a better life, its deeply embedded illusion of self-improvement. We needed it. These men and women, with stomachs they had long since given up on restraining behind thick belts, their polyester-blend slacks, their cardigans littered with an infestation of pills, their baseball hats and harsh growths of facial hair, were damaged goods in comparison to the GAP clothes and the SPIN haircuts of the kids. Loose jeans and baggy sport jackets trickled past Marjorie's table, not registering the presence of Howard and Edna and Ron. My fellow oldster classmates looked like kitchen staff on a break. I actually was kitchen staff on a break. I sat down with them, finally, because I was tired of being invisible.

Anyway, they looked like they were having a good time. Howard had just broken out laughing, a loud cow bellow that showed his small teeth in his bubble-gum-pink gums. "How long have you been here?" Howard asked. He was the one in the baseball hat; golden block letters spelled out the battleship *Nimitz* across the bubble of his forehead. He wore a T-shirt, and a blue cardigan and tight new blue jeans. I saw as he adjusted his hat that, what I had mistaken for a thin watch band, was really a cord of raw hide with a large turquoise amulet. He laughed and said, "You can only be young once."

"But it sure lasts a long time," I said.

I was cramming for another class in archeology one day, and this woman with incredibly long, black hair kept turning her head and filling my textbooks with fine, black strands. I'd gently sweep it away. It smelled like some sort of flower—at this point I hadn't had sex in maybe four years—the two years in prison where I'd thankfully avoided sex and the two years before that when I had been married to my coke-jacked adrenaline rush. Now I'd been clean and exercising. I felt twenty-five and I was surrounded by twenty-year-old girls who had just moved to their own apartments. She kept getting her hair in my book. Finally I said, "Excuse me, Miss, you keep getting your hair in my book."

"What? Don't you like my hair?" she had turned around in her seat. Now, she wasn't gorgeous or anything, but she was a nice kid.

"It's lovely," I said. "But I'm trying to study."

"Suit yourself."

Three minutes later, I had a book full of hair again. I pulled hard enough on her hair that she gasped. "Sorry," I said.

The other oldsters noticed what had happened in class, and I could tell Marjorie was furious. Her husband had left her for a much younger woman. "These young cunts only want one thing—money. As soon as she finds out you work at a grill and drink like a fish, she's out of there."

"Do I look like I want a date?"

"Yes," she said as she zipped her backpack. "But I don't date drunks."

I thought about the young girl for three days even

though I knew I should have been thinking about Marjorie while I worked the grill during the evening. I drew out a mental diagram; Marjorie represented sobriety, a future, and a woman who been places, while the girl represented drunkenness, youth, and no future. That was hard to argue against, because when that no-future finally rolled around, I'd just be back to where I was now. I smoked through my last cigarette break, started scraping the wide grill plate as the waitresses began to pack up the tables. I walked home, showered for a long time, the whole after-work routine a familiar and constant movement, so familiar that I didn't have to think, I just kept it up and kept moving. Three days after the hair incident, I followed the girl across the campus. Her butt was really flat, but she had a waist narrow as the neck of a Coca-Cola bottle. "Hey," I said.

She turned and looked over the grassy slope where I had stopped her. Other students crossed the space with books in their arms or lugging heavy backpacks on one shoulder. I could see Marjorie standing with Howard and Edna near the door to the history portable.

"Are you like stalking me?"

"No. I was just wondering if you'd go to dinner with me."

"Yeah, sure. I never have plans for Wednesday. Wednesday?"

"That would be good."

"And a movie."

"I'm not really up for dinner and a movie. Unless you like to talk your way through the movie."

"No, I don't really like people who talk in movies. When I saw *White Nights* I had the manager kick this couple out who were sitting in front of me and kept complaining about Baryshnikov."

"I was kicked out of *White Nights* for complaining about that commie dancer; what's his name?"

"Baryshnikov?" She laughed. "You're stupid." She dropped her bag, and pulled a pen out of the pocket on the side of her bag. She wrote her number and address and apartment number on a slip of paper that turned out to be an ATM slip. She had three hundred and eighteen dollars in her account, and the slip said five dollars had been drawn out that morning at eight-thirty. Five dollars. Only a fucking twenty-year-old college kid would pay seventy-five cents to draw out five bucks. I looked back for Marjorie. I was having second thoughts about getting involved in all the stupid shit I did when I was twenty, but Marjorie was the only one to know what was good for her and had already headed for cover.

A month later, this was the scene: I lay on the floor of the girl's parent's house. I couldn't remember her name or her parents' names. Her parents were my age, lawyers or something. They'd been out of town for a month and would be back in a week. I'd been working on a bottle of Canadian whiskey that someone had brought to the three-week-old party. Friends her age had passed out long ago. If I hadn't had a liver and metabolism conditioned by three hundred years of alcoholism, I'd have been out long before. Instead I was laying on the floor remembering what the world had looked like when I was kid. I used to spend most of my time on the floor staring up at the bottom of tables, up at the ceiling of our home in Seattle, a house from the turn of the century with elaborate designs in the acoustic tiles. At the girl's house, I lay in front of this thing, this artwork installation piece of crap, an obvious status symbol of how much money their family could afford to waste. Here they were with this lovely house that we'd trashed and a lovely daughter who'd slept even with me. Most of the young boys at the party had screwed her. At one time in the course of the festivities I had found myself in a room of thrown-off boyfriends. "Why are we here?" one of the young guys was saying. "She's even slept with him!" He had stuck out a long finger at me. "It's not fucking polite to point," I had said.

I lay on the floor, one of the only awake people in the house when in walks the girl and a girlfriend I'd never seen before. The bottle of whiskey sat next to me, but I had gradually become so two-dimensional that even the bottle was too tall for me to grab. "Art?" the girl asked me. "Art, the party has been over for three days. Jesus Christ." This sweet girl and her friend had to carry me to the sink, a beautiful porcelain hippy sink, handmade with fat purple cartoon earthworms wriggling over the whole thing. They lay me face down in the sink, my legs draped down to the floor.

She asked me, "What is this sink attached to?"

"My fucking asshole."

"No." She leaned on my back, pressing my chest painfully into the edge of the counter.

"The sewer?"

"Good. Correct." She poured the rest of the bottle down the sink. "And you keep drinking this stuff, that's where you're going." She lifted the bottle up, curling her back, and hurled the bottle down. The hard rim of the bottle bottom slammed into the hand-fired porcelain. The entire sink basin smashed. We watched as huge chucks of porcelain bounced on the tile floor and big shards shattered and other pieces whizzed under the table and into the next room.

There I was at the sewage lagoon, where I had eaten the fruit grown from the soil gathered from the drain pipes and sewer mains. I could barely see the treatment plant across the old farm fields, through the low-lying clouds and dim morning light.

I opened the door of the Subaru and stood to stretch on the pavement next to the car. Flattened splotches of gum had accumulated on the asphalt, some so old that the white skin had cracked and peeled. I grabbed my backpack from the floor of the passenger side and walked down to the muddy Snohomish River. The cold river curled away into the fog along the parking lot. In the misty light, I couldn't see anything around the surface of the water. An eighteen-wheeler screamed on the I-5 overpass floating somewhere way above the river in all that fog. The noise settled back to the slapping river water on the undercut clay bank and the almost imperceptible groan of the Snohomish flowing toward Puget Sound. I took off my pants and shirt and underwear as quickly as possible. From my backpack, I took out my Ivory soap and soap case, the one I had used in prison. They made us buy this crap, so I took it with me. I've gotten so used to the ritual of setting my bag down on the sink and washing that I can't imagine how I ever managed before. On top of the pile of my clothes, I lay my folded underwear. I raised the bar of soap into the sky and plunged into the water. I pulled myself onto the bank, put on my jeans, and walked back to the Brat where I put on a warm, dry T-shirt.

I started up the Subaru and took a deep smell of myself. I smelled like river mud and rain water. I wanted to go home and forget everything that had happened to me. I wanted to go home and make sure that Marjorie hadn't given up on me. As I drove home, back to Marjorie, I passed a white farm house. All along the road next to the big mailbox, yellow lantern heads of daffodils hung over the rushing ditch. I stopped and dug around in the back and finally found a knife I'd taken from Denny's to scrape the Subaru's spark plugs. I took a big step over the stream. It was full of swiftly running water that pulled the long blades of green grass along. I looked at the house. It had that early morning look, all the lights were off, the chimney was still, water rolled down the window panes, and I knew that I had gotten an early enough start for once. I leaned into that bed of cold flower stalks and cut down six daffodils, getting the sticky flower blood all over my hands. It smelled rich and sweet and I knew if I hurried I could get home before Marjorie woke up. She'd wake up and there'd be eggs cooking and fresh flowers that her man had home brought home to her after his morning swim.

Instructions For Running

———•———

My boss, name of Ross Hayden, really liked the way I handled his business. When the shipping trucks were three days late and our entire supply of white cement ran out, I kept everything in order. At closing time, just as the clock whistle began to blow, the trucks rolled into the parking lot and cruised right through the gate, almost hitting one of the part-time guys trying to close the chain-link doors. The Kenmore trucks sat in the lot with their lights beaming into the storeroom and Ross ran around shouting at them. "Three days you're late, and I've got all my guys already going home. What in the hell am I supposed to do?"

"It's all right, boss; I can handle it. I'll make sure we have things where we need them." I rattled the keys to the warehouse. "You go home and get dinner. This is handled. When you come back tomorrow, everything will be just fine." After he left, I worked for two hours getting the flats of cement into the warehouse. I cut the shipping wire and hauled the jangling strips of metal to the trash. In the morning, when Ross and the other guys came in, they just looked at the stuff I had done on my own time and they just shook their heads.

I could get a customer to do anything. For instance, this joker pulled up in a pickup truck that he must have modified himself; the thing supported a plywood house built on the back, painted barn red with white trim. I could tell he would be trouble as soon as he dropped out of the truck and slammed his door. He hitched his belly over his belt buckle, a brass-plated disc that read *The Potholes 1977*, and threw open the barn doors on the back of his pickup truck, letting out some sort of music with accordions and horns. Lumber that the warehouse had discontinued months ago, filled the truck bed. "I want to make a return," he said.

"Sorry, sir," I said, "but we can't take back this merchandise as it has been discontinued." I saved the man the trouble of closing his barn doors and closed them myself.

He said, "I have my receipt." He shook it in front of my face so fast I couldn't tell whether it was a piece of paper or a pom-pom.

"If you would read our return policy, we won't take anything that has been discontinued. Your merchandise has been discontinued. Sorry." The man rolled the paper up into his fist. He flung open one of the barn doors. Inside I could see shelves with old paint cans and tools and gasoline drums just sitting there where they could explode if anything set them off. Before I could tell him what a moving disaster his barn was, the man turned back to me. He said, "Go on, take them. I bought them here, and I'm going to return them here. You're the guys who took my money."

At this point, Ross appeared on the scene. He said in his silky, *I am the manager and I'm here to please you like no one else can,* voice "Can I do something for you?"

"This guy," Potholes said, "won't take back my lumber even though I've got a receipt."

Ross looked at the receipt and handed it back to Potholes. "Looks fine. Milton, help this man unload his lumber."

"Sure," I said. The man rolled his tongue around in his mouth as I flung open the barn door. I dropped the tailgate. I started to slide the sheets of mahogany plywood from the back. At about half-way, I palmed my pocketknife and scratched a gash on the first board and then I did that with the rest of the sheets. I kept my body over the wood as I worked. On one hand, I don't know exactly why I did this. On the other hand, it did exactly what I wanted. He had to keep his lumber and we didn't have to unload it.

Potholes stood behind me. "What's taking you so long," he said. "They heavy?"

"I just saw something in here, lard-ass." That's when he looked at me. He began to assess me. Before that, I had been some sort of flunky, but now who I actually was dropped in front of him like one of those character cards in *Dick Tracy*. He saw that the weight of these pieces of wood was nothing for arms like mine. He could see that I could swing his fat guts over my shoulder by his ankles and bash his head off against the side of the his barn. His head would snap off his body like a Ken doll. I pulled the panel out. "It's got a two foot scratch? How are we supposed to take these back?"

"I don't know," Potholes said.

"We won't," I said.

I slid his outdated, gaudy lumber back into his truck. I slammed the doors as he left. As he drove off he didn't burn rubber or anything.

Ross wanted to know where the guy was going. I shook

my head. "That lumber was discontinued. But you knew that."

"Sure," Ross said. "Sure." He looked at me, checking my head, my shoes, everything. "Your shirt needs to be untucked," he said. "And get your hands dirty, you're supposed to be working around here." He watched as I pulled my neatly tucked shirt out of my Levis.

I've taken control of my life, not that it was a wreck, but I grew up with parents that were always on the move. I slept in so many different rooms and places as a child, that I needed a certain afghan to fall asleep. It had a motif of the Pony Express on it. I could wrap myself in this blanket anywhere, and suddenly I would be in my room. In school I was the new kid and, many times, the kids in my classes didn't know my name too well. They didn't even really see me. Now people can't help but notice me. I work out daily. I run around a track three times a week. I read the bestsellers.

Ross never saw me. Even a dick-headed customer like Potholes saw me. Even women who didn't know me saw me; at least the ones who were unimportant to me. Sometimes, when I went out drinking after work with a few of my friends from shipping, a woman's eyes, just beginning to gloss, swept across the bar and I knew she really saw me. She noticed the way my shoulders fed into my arms, the extension of my triceps—and if she was familiar with body building, familiar with power, she couldn't help but notice that the arms under my T-shirt were legit.

The smoke choked me in those places. One time, my friends and I sat around a small table. We sort of stood while we leaned against these too tall stools. We couldn't even see to the next table through the blue haze of cigarette smoke. I caught glimpses, through the gradual breaks in the mist, of the next table; several women had filled the table top and the ledge behind them with empty glasses. The glasses reminded me of the milky white-glass figurines my grandmother collected in her bedroom, so many hoarded through her life that when she finally died we couldn't give the things away; instead we rolled them into toilet paper and left them in a cardboard box in the attic of the house she had been renting. These women had all the fancy glasses, the kind that looked like upsidedown bells, the tall, skinny kind that opened toward the top like stretched flowers. It took me a while to get all this through the rolling clouds of smoke. I slapped one of my buddies on the arm. He couldn't hear me under the noise of the music, the bartender shouting *sour up!* and the cocktail waitress careening through the small islands of tables, beer foam spilling down her arms as she screamed *Excuse me! 'scuse me!* My buddy grabbed my arm and I half pulled him out of the chair for trying to muscle me. He tipped his head at the next table. "Hos!" He shouted but in the racket it sounded like a whisper.

I walked by the table with the women, checking out their black skirts, bulky gold necklaces, earrings—visible through the murk of smoke like fishing lures in muddy water—and halos of hair lifted unnaturally from their scalps with sprays, mousses, and gels. Their hair caught the light like distant moons. I caught one of them looking at me, examining me with the standard head-to-toe route. She made stops, I knew, at my jaw line, at my shoulders, and my mid-section. Slight love handles sat just above my belt line; actually, as handles go, they weren't big. Sometimes when I'd work out I thought I should just cut the crap and work them out. Inevitably it occurred to me— why the fuck bother? This woman, for instance, stopped at the sag of my flesh-filled shirt and I knew what she thought; she believed I was a generous guy. I had a soft spot, maybe a little too visible, but something she was going to catch.

I took a swing around the bar and walked back to the island of women. The one looked at me again. When I sat down at the table my buddy shouted into my ear. "Well? What's the action?"

"Shit," I said, "all shit." I grabbed a cocktailer who stumbled by our table and ordered a Mai-Tai for the woman who had scoped me out. Before the cocktailer turned away, I changed the order to a White Russian; I decided to make her a White Russian kind of woman.

Ten minutes later, the cocktailer brushed by our table and shouted to me, "She says come by her table."

I sat next to the woman and I saw she was somewhere in her twenties. Her eyes had starter wrinkles and her make-up—too much, too neat—made her look like one of those dolls with a hard face, whose eyes follow you across toy stores. Her lips glowed bright red. They ended abruptly in the white polish of her skin. She didn't have a single exposed mole. I couldn't see her body. I figured I would find out. I said some things that made her laugh while I checked her out. Her friends had their backs to us, three boxy shadows with glowing heads of hair.

"We should go outside to talk better." I said this and gestured toward the walls to make her understand.

She nodded and leaned into her friends. She stood and I saw her body. Nothing bad or exciting, the kind of body you'd expect on someone who sat behind a desk all day.

I dropped some cash with my buddy, then the woman and I walked outside to the covered sidewalk. Wet cars filled the parking lot. Beyond the lot I saw the marquee for the movies, the letters not quite visible through the rain. She picked me because of my love handles. She knew

I wouldn't be put off when I pulled off her bra and her tits sagged into the folds of her stomach. She could loosen up a little around a guy like me. We laughed on the way to my apartment. She laughed extremely weird, it sounded like one of those hobo musicians playing a woodsaw. But I didn't care because her face was so tidy that I didn't have to think about the way she would look when we banged. I already knew.

I was seeing a woman. I saw her twice a week. I didn't know her name. But I called her Betsy. I'd thought about how sex would be with Betsy. First of all, Betsy was not just a stranger. Second of all, I'd thought about doing things with Betsy, like going to Seattle and walking around the Pike Place Market, me buying her some cherries or something and her sitting on the terrace that overlooks Puget Sound, the cold, salty wind rushing over our faces. Betsy and I had a built-in history. She was the only girl who was any goodlooking who walked at the track. I always said, "Hey, Betsy," when she passed me. I knew she must've liked me because every time I saw her at the track she always faced me. This meant that she just happened to walk in such a way that we always looked into each other's eyes. Something was going to happen. Me and her. I could feel it.

I depended on seeing her at the track. I needed a witness. People had to see me at the daily task of exercise so I would show up and accumulate my effort into the hard roll of my biceps, in the cut tendons of my calves, my strength. Be seen: this was my sole instruction. At the track, I nodded at the same people every day and at the gym I high-fived my buddies. These things, this expected routine, kept me going, and I acquired witnesses who acknowledged the control I had over my body and my life.

Besides Betsy, I always ran past an old couple leashed to their dog. I ran past a guy who wasn't a weight lifter. His chest was shallow. His shoulders only looked buff because he swung his arms so goddamn hard as he ran around the track. Even with such a butt-ugly face and wimped-out torso he still waved at Betsy every time he passed her.

I ran by her. Mr. Wimp and I ran in tandem around the track. Sometimes I started to gain on him. I followed the silky hang of his red athletic shorts as they swung back and forth. I moved toward him, legs pounding the cinder track, spitting red clods of dirt along the backs of my legs. I jogged next to him and whispered, "Don't talk to my Betsy." But he didn't hear me because I spoke just under my breath, and the words came out like *huff huff huff* don't talk *huff* to my *huff huff* Betsy. He didn't. Keeping himself away from her as he left, he contained himself to a small wag of his hand like an imitation of Queen Elizabeth visiting Washington DC.

Betsy smiled at me.

I knew what her footprints in the track looked like. After it rained the cinder was smoothed and I liked to show up at the track, the first man to make my mark. And then she showed up in her yellow Civic and I watched her feet leave a trail of size seven footprints.

After it rained, the wall of windows that used to be the cafeteria at Woodrow Wilson High School sparkled and reflected the length of the old track, the distant fence, and the closed-down cement factory across the street. Four hundred freakishly unbroken panes stretched over the wall. I liked to look at myself as I ran around the track.

From being a distant figure on the far side of the loop, I would come to the unwashed panes and my image would grow; I floated across the glass, a grey, long-legged shadow, and finally I would turn my back to the wall of windows. I thought of cleaning Woodrow Wilson's windows; I thought of buying fifteen or sixteen spray bottles of Windex and going at the windows, like one of those berserk warriors in *Thor* who were supposed to go to Valhalla after they slaughtered everything in their path. I would clean every window in my path, wiping, spraying, cleaning. But I realized that after I cleaned the windows, they would be clear. In the sunlight the windows would show the empty and dusty space behind them; they would show the green and faded tiles of the cafeteria under a layer of left-behind Styrofoam cups, aluminum cans, and school milk cartons. They wouldn't reflect me. I used to sit in that room with my friends and even some girls when the school was new. It's not that way now. I don't like to think about the time that separates the two things—the me then and the me now.

Even so, I keep in touch with my little brother Dillon. He's what I could've been like, if I hadn't took it on myself to get things learned by myself. I wouldn't have considered dropping school when my mother asked me to leave. Anyway, things turned out pretty good. I have my work.

As a sixteen-year-old freshmen at Wilson High I worked full to part time at a gas station fixing cars and trucks. I worked all night at a gas station on Pacific Highway South. I would go into the station with a six pack of RC Cola and lay under the belly of rundown Fords and go to town on them. The men I worked with always dressed in blue jump suits with so much grease accumulated in the fabric that when they sat down on the garage chair they left pools of oil. These guys always had a lit cigarette sticking out of their mouth. I joked with them that if they dropped a match they would burn like a junkyard tire fire. They would burn and burn and no matter what we did, spray them with the special chemical fire retardant in its florescent yellow fire extinguisher, no matter what, they would burn until they turned as brown and dark and boiled as the backside of a rusted out Ford pickup truck.

"You're a handsome guy," my mother told me one night before I moved out for good, "and you work full time. When you left the first time, I didn't think I would see you for a while. I thought you were about to go out into the world and make room for yourself."

"I did," I said, "there's just not room enough for me, yet."

"You got a lot going for you, Milton," she said. She took my hands and looked at me. We were both smoking Marlboro's—her cigarettes—she smoked anything a man smoked. She had Camel wrappers all over the back of her crappy Ford that I usually spent my days off fixing. We didn't say anything. We just sat looking at each other's smoke swirl and then I looked outside at the parking lot of the apartment building she had moved into, at the Nova missing a headlight, at the Caprice Classic spray-painted black. She had lived for a while at a place in Carnation along the Snoqualmie River after she left Dad. Now we lived here, close to her job at Ed's #1 Diner on First Avenue South.

I had bought a Chevy—1972 Malibu, lime green. I planned on fixing it. Now I sat at the table with my mother and she told me I had to go. She summed up how well I could take care of myself when she finally added, "and you have a sweet auto."

"What about your car? It ain't sweet and it's not auto—it needs me." That crappy car needed more than me, it needed its own full-time, fully-staffed garage. Fucking Ford.

"I can manage. Nathan can fix it if it breaks down." Nathan was her boyfriend. He didn't live here then, thank God, but I could maybe see why she wanted me gone. She wanted me out of the house so Nathan could move into her place and Dillon could move the hell out of the living room into my old bedroom. Without me, they could have people over and watch TV, play cards, whatever the fuck normal people did with their living room. All Dillon did of any use was read. My brother Dillon went to school and came home with nothing to do but watch TV and read from his school books. Now, when he shows up at my apartment, he always has a book in his hands, even though he is well out of college. He gets paid less than me which might account for him wanting to drink the beer I pay for.

"In a place of your own," Mom said, "you can have anything you like. You can do anything you like. You're the one who's always making sure this place is vacuumed, cleaned and spit-shined. I'm not here to do that. In your own place I won't be there to screw it up."

"Another reason I should stay, I fix your car *and* I clean up your house."

"Nope. One—I don't need the house cleaned up by you, because you throw all kinds of shit out—shit I'm saving. Two—the car is taken care of. Three—if you won't take a hint, Mr. Milton, you're old enough not to be living with your mother."

"I'm sixteen."

"You turn seventeen in four months."

"Okay. I'm gone." She thought she could take care of

herself. I had taken care of her for seventeen years.

I left the gas station and her crappy apartment. I meant to call. I didn't though—out of sight out of mind—and we didn't talk. My perpetual excuse was work.

I had to keep them happy at work. Sometimes Ross would start firing people and anyone could go; even when one of my buddies who had worked in shipping with me ran half an hour late after a night of drinking, Ross fired him. Ross just looked at him. "Fired," he said.

I kept things in good shape for him. I made certain I did that. I even went into sections I didn't normally work. The nuts, bolts, and rivets section almost always needed ordering. Screws had specific widths, measured in millimeters separated into plainly marked bins. Anyone could see that this woman didn't belong in the fastener section with her painted finger nails and her dress flapping up and down the aisles. She mixed the screws like she was preparing hors d'oeuvres by following the directions on the back of a box of Chex. She threw the 1.50s into the 2.0s. She mixed the Phillips head screws with the straight head screws. She screwed everything up.

I saw her reach into a bin and hold a handful of metal in her hand, walk halfway down the aisle, and then hold one of the screws up to her eyes like the magnification would mean something. She dropped the whole handful into a bin of nails.

I approached her. I tapped her on the shoulder and told her politely to leave. "Ma'am," I said, "You're going to have to leave."

"Hello," she said. "Do you work here? I can't find a Phillips head screw like this one."

I held the screw up to my eye. The screw she handed me had been cross threaded, a wreck. It looked like 1.5 mm, Phillips. "You're looking for one item?"

"Yeah."

"You've just cost us about three hours of painstaking labor to re-sort all the screws you've just dropped in the bins. We don't need your three cents worth of business, if you'll pardon the expression."

"Pardon it? Sure, I'll pardon," she said. She smiled at me. She strolled down the aisle and I started sorting. Four hours later, after I found that someone must have gone through every bin and mixed everything, Ross tapped me on the shoulder. "Hey," I said.

"What're you doing over here?"

"The screws are screwed," I said.

"So I've been told," he said. "You ever see this?" He handed me the trashed Phillips-head screw the woman had been looking for.

"No," I said. "Looks like some kid has been playing construction man." Ross could say nothing to that.

I pressed my fingers into the dusty red cinders of the old track while I stretched. Pansy Runner ran past me while I rolled my neck in circles. His butt jiggled under his nylon shorts and his shoulders rotated with his hips. I went through my routine twice before Betsy pulled up in her Honda. As I heard her car door slam, I started running around the track. "Hey, Betsy," I said. Nothing. Nylon Butt waved and she said something to him. I heard him chuckling ahead of me, a sound like Dillon would make after a joke that he only understood on account of his going to college.

I passed Betsy again. Nothing. My toes tingled and the instep of my foot began to grow hot and blister under my tight shoe laces. I began to gain on Nylon Dick. I watched the triangle of his foot pull back. The roll of his calf jiggled up and then fell as his foot planted down. The foot flew back and then as it started to plant I kicked the heel in a straight point, the way I used to kick soccer balls. He fell. He rolled into the old football field where he lay still. I kept running. When I came back around to where he had fallen, Betsy was helping him to his feet and holding him up. She glanced up at me. I nodded. She didn't do anything but look into Nylon Dick's face. He drew his lips into a flat smile and they walked over to the parking lot together.

I kept running. On each pass I would stare at myself in the wall of windows and raise my eyebrows. Who knew he would fall? The pansy.

After work, Dillon called. "Hey, I'm coming over," he said.

"What for?" I asked. I was doing my dishes. I had to run to the store to get a new vacuum cleaner belt because I had worn it out and had used the extra. "I've got plans," I told Dillon. He sounded like he was on a pay phone. I could hear the sound of a motor running. Car doors slammed. People murmured things just beyond the mouthpiece.

"I'm already on my way over," he said.

I started looking for things Dillon might see when he came over. I decided to stand at the door. He didn't have to come in. The futon with the red comforter needed to be refolded across the back. The press board bookcases needed dusting. The carpet needed to be vacuumed.

When Dillon knocked, I stood in front of the door. "I have to come in," he said as he pressed the door into my chest. "I've got to go," he said.

"No," I said. "The place is a sty." I held the dust rag in my hand. I hadn't finished.

"I'll close my eyes," Dillon said. "I'm your brother; you've got to let me in."

"Close your eyes," I said. I waited for him outside the bathroom, casually dusting the door's molding. When Dillon saw me standing in the hallway with the rag, he said, "It's okay. You've still got some toilet paper in there." I shoved the rag into the coat closet and when I turned around I caught Dillon spiraling through my apartment. He fell across the futon, knocking the folded red comforter on the floor. I sat down on my sofa. "What's going on?" I said.

"Work," Dillon said, "work all day."

He looked at me. I looked at him. "Let's get some beer," Dillon said.

We drove around after we picked up some chilled beer. We stopped just as it started to turn dark at a lake way out beyond Seattle, out toward the mountains, along miles and miles of tree-lined roads. At the park, we sat on the cold grass. The sky turned dark. Then Dillon said, "Let's go out to the raft."

"Why?"

"I don't know," he said. "Let's go." We lay out in the raft, beyond my job, beyond his work, sauced, together looking at the trees around us, and then the faint stars that appeared in the sky above us. Around us the sharp shapes of the trees hanging over the lake looked like a couple of gates guarding us. I remembered, lying with my back pressed to the warm wood, a time when Dad had taken Dillon and me way up into the mountains to swim at a lake. I had just learned to swim the winter before at the YMCA. The lake filled up the entire floor of a valley. Old rotting logs choked up the side of the lake. Dad told me to help him push one of these logs out into the middle of the lake with him. "Like a raft," he said.

"It will be in the middle of the lake," I said. We were paddling beside this log. A few bushes grew along the exposed side of the log and it bobbed in the water beside us.

"Look," Dad said. "If we get tired on the way, we can just rest on the log." We paddled and pushed the log to the middle of the lake and it sank. I don't know, on recalling it, how it could have floated at all.

As the log slowly vanished into the bluish depths below us, I asked, "What do we do now?"

"Swim to shore."

"Which way?" I asked, because we were in the middle of this lake. But Dad was already swimming back toward Dillon. Dillon stood on the shore waving his arms. My arms started to ache on the way back and my head dipped under water.

On the raft, by the beach, I reminded Dillon about the log that sank and how Dad had left me in the middle of the lake.

"That must have sucked," Dillon said.

"Don't you remember that?"

"You made it to shore."

"Barely," I said. We made the mistake of getting dry, lying out there; when we stood up to go back to where our clothes lay on the beach, we just looked at the rolling silver waves with the white specks of insects skittering over the surface.

"How are we going to get back?" I asked.

"What am I supposed to do," Dillon said, "Swim?"

We dared each other, and then he pushed me, and I pulled him, and we fell backward into the lake. My skin hit the cold surface and then I was under it into the warm body of water. I surfaced out of the greenish depths, and I swam with Dillon beside me toward our clothes.

I woke with my face in the carpet. The strands that pressed into my face tasted like a toothbrush someone had been cleaning their shoes with, plastic and dirty.

Dillon sat on the edge of my futon. "Hey," he said, "wake up, don't you work today?" He was dressed in his work clothes.

I jumped into the shower, shaving with one hand while lathering my hair with the other hand. "See yah," Dillon said. When I finally looked at the clock I was well past the point of making it to work on time. I called in sick to cover my ass.

I went to the track, thinking about Betsy. When I finally got there, I waited. I sat in the car all morning, watching Nylon Butt run around the track, and then the old couple being dragged around by their dog. Finally, hours after she should have shown up, hours after I should have been at work, she did show up. Her Honda parked and then she walked around the track alone. She waved her arms back and forth as she walked, the black line of her Walkman cord flipping up and down.

I jumped out of the Chevy and slipped around the track. "Hey, Betsy," I said, even though she wore head phones. She didn't say anything. She pretended I didn't exist. It was like I wasn't even there. And then the next lap around I waved with a soft, limp flap of my hand and I was around the track again. On the next loop, I tackled her. I brought my chest up into her torso, and then lowered her. As I closed into her I could smell the shampoo floral smell of her hair unfurling around my head and I heard the tinny racket of her head phones. She didn't scream like I had expected her to. Then I had my fingers in her mouth, and I felt her cold damp tongue between my index and middle finger.

Finally I had her around the back, and I tossed her into her Honda. I slammed the door shut and asked her for her keys.

She sat next to me just breathing. The windows started

to fog almost at once. We sat in the parking lot. I looked around to see if anyone had noticed, but the traffic drove past the school and no one did anything. "Do you know who I am?" I yelled at her as she suddenly started to scramble for the door. I hit her on the head until she sat still in her seat. She did not answer me.

When she looked at me then, her eyes were like two brown, flat M&Ms. "Rapist," she said. As I raised my hand to hit her, I thought, I should just bang the bitch and get on with it. But I couldn't. I had an erection but it just made me feel sick. So I let her be in her foggy little shelled-out Honda Civic. I hopped into my Chevy Malibu. I peeled, burned rubber for as long as the car would stay on it, and then I was out into the traffic.

I slept. When the clock radio began, it was in the middle of a song, *four three two one,* someone sang. *Earth below us floating weightless.* I remembered the video; guitars sound as sections of a rocket fell back toward the earth. I pulled the plug on my clock, set to go off early enough to get me to the track before work. Finally, when I felt like it, I headed into work.

When I pulled into the office the cashiers, who usually didn't arrive until an hour after I had started, were already standing in their row. Some of them smiled at me. "Ross is looking for you."

"Haven't been feeling well," I said.

"He misses you, sweetheart," the cashier said.

"Hey, Milton man," Ross said, sweeping down one of the aisles. "Good to see you. Glad you decided to drop in today. You can drop in next week to pick up your check. Why don't you go on back home."

"For what?"

"You're fired."

I didn't know what to do. I left, thinking that if I went home and let Ross cool off that I could get my position back. On the way home, as I began to realize that wasn't the case, I brought three twenty-eight-ounce spray bottles of Windex from the Food Merchant. I don't know why I bought the Windex. But it made me feel a little better.

Dillon sat outside my apartment door reading one of his books. He wore a brand new green sweat shirt and black jeans. He had on new shoes. "Hey," he said. He started going through my grocery bag. "What's this Windex for?"

"To clean windows," I told him.

"Your windows are clean," he said.

We sat at my table. I didn't ask him how or why he was in my apartment. "I wanted to clean these windows at the high school," I said. "Four hundred unbroken panes," I said.

"Four hundred unbroken panes?"

"Yeah."

"Let's break them," he said.

When he said that, I thought of the absence of those windows, and how it would look to run around the track and expect to look up and see myself running and running and not see anything. How would I know I was doing it?

Dillon and I cruised around looking for rocks. Finally we found a place on the Cedar River, just up from Renton Stadium. We tossed handful of rocks into my laundry hamper and then hauled it back to my Chevy. Six trips and the back of my car practically sanded off on my tires.

As it began to get dark the sunlight shined in an angle across the field, turning everything orange. Dillon and I rolled out onto the track and I backed the car up. "Just throw a rock," I yelled. "You can't miss." I could see myself in the wall of windows that reflected Dillon and me. As I drew my arm back, my mirror double drew its arm back. In an instant it would shatter. I almost yanked my shoulder out of its socket as I let the stone fly.

Sleep Dummy

———◆———

I ran into Nathan Anderson, an old friend, at the Seattle
Art Museum at a travelling exhibition of an artist I had
never heard of, Edward Hopper, but judging from the
reaction of the people walking through the rooms I guess
he was pretty famous. I came on these paintings that
terrified me. In one painting there was a woman—she
looked like a needle freak with yellow skin, except she
had too much meat on her bones—who gazing out the
window beyond the frame. Light from the portrait's window fell on her haggard face. She sat on the bed looking
out the window. For me that picture portrayed every morning after.

A man stood in front of the painting like a child looking into the Christmas window display at the Frederick &
Nelson department store. He was short and skinny. I could
tell he had muscles under his tight black T-shirt and his
faded Levis. He wore a huge belt buckle of a snake eating
its own tail that I think was a vintage artifact from the
early seventies. His face, lined and flat, had a healthy color,
even though he was thin as a knife.

I remembered a man who had worn a belt buckle like the one this guy was wearing, and I realized then that this was Nathan, who I knew years ago, when I first moved to Seattle. He and I had once hit it off. I don't know whether it was because we were drinking rum and smoking reefer or because there was a physical attraction—I was a little too gone to recall—but we lost track of whose drink was whose after I accidentally drank from his glass and left a red lipstick smear on the rim. After that, we drank from both glasses. After we were toasted he said, "Janice baby, let's get drunk together," which frankly meant, "let's get roaring obnoxious and fuck." After a joint and another glass of rum chased with a couple of beers, we made it back to my apartment. We stumbled into my soft bed, we pulled the warm sheets over our heads and, well, we weren't in the position to say "no," or much of anything else. We woke at sunrise and drank coffee in the indistinct gray light that came out of the mid-winter Seattle sky.

As we sat on my couch with the rancid coffee I had prepared with three scoops of tinned grounds, Nathan wrapped his arm around me and held me so tight that I had difficulty raising the cup to my lips. "Quit it," I said, happy to have some one to be grumpy with.

It had been a rough six or seven weeks the winter I dropped out of college; actually I dropped out of attempting to save money for college. Things like rent and groceries took everything I earned running around the tables of the Red Diner downtown. I stayed up late partying, and found a million men, with their deep belly buttons under black curled hair, their fatty muscles, and the deep salty smell of their arm pits attractive enough that they would find their way back to my place. In all of these cases they would wake before dawn and dress in the dark. Leaning down, they kissed me and lied to me at the same time; smacking their lips as they left, they said the mantra that would start another day for me, "I'll call you." And sometimes they would. But they never lay in bed with me and waited long enough for me to make some coffee and lay with me on the sofa and sort out the time of the day like Nathan had done.

I suppose that I wouldn't remember all of these things— the long winter, the succession of guys, and the few times with Nathan—if I had never missed my period. When it finally stopped, I bought a bottle of red wine and a urine test at Fred Meyer, aware as I paid the old woman behind the counter—a woman who was much older than Mom when Mom finally died—that the cashier knew it wasn't good news that I had to buy something like this. A man who buys a urine test is a good thing, but a woman who does it, that is just bad news. At home I took the test and drank the red wine to celebrate the positive. I didn't even know when the last time I had a period was, so I found a friend who had a friend who knew a doctor and got it cleaned out before I started thinking about pink or blue pajamas with the special vinyl foot pads.

Nathan stopped by an oil painting of what from the other side of the room looked like a watchtower overlooking a blood red battlefield, but when I came close I saw that it was really just a railway station at the edge of a sunset. "Nathan?" I said. I tried for a friendly, *Hello it's been years* tone of voice. But who can control these things? My voice cracked, and then in an effort to cover it up, I said, "It's been some time." Which came out in clear, slow syllables.

He turned around and I thought, "Oh fuck, I've never seen this man in my life." His face was so thin that I could see the arc of his skull in his forehead. But he smiled and said, "Janice?"

I don't know, but recognition from someone who hasn't seen me in almost twenty years—this was a gift. If he had suddenly reached into his pocket and wrapped a twisty wire from the grocery store around my finger and proposed, I would have married him even though I know what all of that is about.

We went to coffee and I realized then that Nathan had not aged as well as I had thought. We talked about my job. We talked about some of the people we knew in common. We hit it off decently enough. But I could tell something was bugging him. He was so skinny and he ate so little. He ordered a hamburger with two slices of cheese, and he ordered an extra side of fries, and then he ate all of his fries and he ate the cheese off his hamburger. He drank the Coke, and he drank six cups of coffee. Bathroom city. We talked about the people we had known all those years ago. When I maneuvered the conversation to the present, talking about the fall of the Soviet Union, or the new Museum downtown, or whatever, his interest would tail off. He would watch someone on the street and say something about her hair. When we talked about what we would do next, he said, "Actually, I have an appointment."

He did ask for my number. But that was only the polite thing to do.

I, however, was getting too old to be polite, and I was attracted to him. One of the things that attracted me to him were the stories I had heard from our mutual friend, Paul Lane, of the abuse Nathan had put himself through, drinking until the bars collapsed behind him, pushing his endurance with whatever powder or capsule or paste was available. He had lived high on the hog, like most people these days just don't. I think, maybe, they look at the wrecks of the seventies, the multitude of vomit-drowned celebrities and the old hippies hanging out in backwoods bars, still wearing love beads even though they have no one to love, and they are afraid. They are afraid of becoming a cultural backwater, of letting things just slip along while they remain in a time and place no one remembers properly, resurrected only in momentary retro styles and spoofy parties. Finding Nathan was like finding a genuine jeans jacket with vintage bead work in a thrift store.

Beyond this, though, I just had the basic motive of wanting to get a real, warm human body into my bed, male and my age preferably.

I still use a body pillow I bought from a flea market the sixth year of my marriage to Art. I call this thing my sleep dummy because it helps me sleep, and with its thick, overstuffed sections it makes me believe I'm sleeping with someone. When I lived with Art, the overstuffed torso usually lay at the foot of our bed. But there were nights when I had to pull it out and lay it in the hollow Art's body usually filled. I had to have the bulk of something there or I just couldn't sleep. Just before I left him I realized that I had been living with the sleep dummy. After work, I'd pull it into Art's spot and then read through my murder mystery and magazines. Finally I would fell sleep. When I woke up in the morning, its head would be resting on my chest; I don't know where Art was, because he wasn't in my bed.

Now I live in an apartment by myself, close to work, and I'm still sleeping with the dummy. Over the years, I've spilled coffee on it. I've dropped ashes on it. It has acquired its own character in the stains and wrinkles and

worn patches. I think of my sleep dummy as the character, Mr. Paterson, from *Tea and Nightshade Murders*. He's
the short, squat, male sleuth who drinks himself to oblivion
while pondering the questions of the murder over his
bottle of sherry. I always say, "Good night, Mr. Paterson,"
before I turn out my light.

I showed up at Nathan's apartment a couple of nights
later with a bottle of wine, spaghetti in a plastic
Tupperware container, and fresh bread. Nathan answered
the door, wearing a bathrobe draped over his thin limbs,
the pale fabric worn and stretched in places his body
wasn't. He was clean-shaven and smelled like lavender bath
crystals, so I assumed there must have been a woman in
his apartment because I couldn't picture him in the bath
tub, floating alone among the white bubbles. I said to
him, "I thought I might drop by, but if you have company..." I was looking past him at the freshly vacuumed
carpet; at the geometric order in the alignment of the
sofa, coffee table, TV; at any sign of a woman, like a compact left on the coffee table, or even something as
conspicuous as two mugs on the table. I didn't see anything. I didn't even hear water running or any other
activity by someone other than Nathan.

   "It's nice to see you," he said, something I was not expecting to hear after his ambivalence at the diner. He
stepped back like he wanted me to come in. The carpet
in his apartment was plush compared to the worn astro-
turf carpet of the hallway. The warm air from the lamp-lit
rooms of Nathan's apartment washed over him, carrying
the lavender smell of his bath and the faint odor of cough
drops or Vick's Vaporub into the bright hallway. I stepped
in. "There is enough for three," I said, as I set the round

Tupperware down in his dark kitchen.

"Three? Did you invite someone?" he said.

"Isn't there someone here?"

"Who would visit me?" and when he said that, at first I was relieved and I almost felt a giddy twitch along my hips. Then I wondered why he felt it was necessary to say something so pathetic.

He turned on the lights in the kitchen to show plain tile counters, empty of the standard appliances, like a toaster or microwave or espresso machine. The only standard thing was a Mr. Coffee. "I need to change, but I'll be right back. There's coffee. Please, sit down." I watched him walk down his hallway, turn into what I assumed was his bedroom and close the door.

Nathan returned wearing a white sweater and slacks. They hung on him. He smiled at me and held out his arms. We hugged and I could feel the ridge of his backbone under the sweater. He groaned and pulled back from me. "You will have to catch me up on everything, including the sordid details of your marriage to what's his name."

"Art."

He stopped and looked at me. "I'm sorry. I can tell that we're getting off to a bad start. First we met like a couple of characters in a bad short story at that Edward Hopper exhibit. I already feel like a manifestation of a cliché. We can get beyond all that after we eat. It's very kind of you to drop by."

"A cliché, what do you mean?"

"I don't know. I just think I've seen that movie too; you know, I've already read that story."

"I'd never seen Hopper's painting before. I liked them."

"They're great," Nathan said. "But you can buy his coffee table book at Costco. I think anything you can buy from a warehouse immediately enters some phase of clichéhood."

"I made my spaghetti from scratch."

"And your sauce?"

"Prego," I said. "From Costco."

"Let me get the wine," he said. "Immediately."

I sat in a square stuffed chair in the living room. The TV was on, but turned to a blue screen. He poured the wine. It gugged and the sharp odor filled the room. "Do we need to heat up the food?"

"It should still be warm."

He placed the wine bottle in the center of the coffee table, and the plate in front of me with an exact motion, like the place was marked with tape. He set the napkin, the fork and knife. "Do you use a knife with noodles?"

"I don't know; do you? You don't use chopsticks," I said. I put one of the couch pillows into my lap, propped my elbows on it and quickly drank the bitter wine.

He set the Tupperware container next to the wine and opened the lid, wafting smells of hamburger and tomato sauce and the pasty Mission noodle odor.

He dumped a mess of noodles and meat sauce on my plate, splattering the table. He took the knife, and gave me his fork. He sat and put half as much as I had on his plate. He wrapped noodles around his knife. Shoving the food into his mouth, he freed his hands to pour more wine. He filled my glass.

I drank the acidic wine. The glass was too full and I slopped some onto the table, where it mixed with the splattered spaghetti.

"Great," he said. "This is just great." He wiped his mouth clean, setting his knife flat on his plate. "This is really good."

I drank my wine in huge gulps. "You don't have to like

it," I said. "To be honest, I'm a really bad cook, and the fact that this spaghetti isn't making you puke on impact is amazing to me."

"No," he said, he raised his eyebrows. "This *is* good."

"You like it then?" I asked.

"Excellent," he said. He made the okay sign with his thumb and forefinger.

I cleaned my fork by sticking it down my mouth, up to the widest point of the handle. I made sure I had Nathan's eye contact. Then I handed him the clean fork. He dropped it on the table. "That's just too sexy," he said.

I pretended for a second to be interested in wiping up the mess of spilled wine and sauce, and then looked up quickly. I caught Nathan spitting out a little of the food. I didn't know what to do. I said, "Are we really going to eat all this? Or are you going to make a pass at me?" I stood up to leave for the bathroom. When I stood, the two glasses of wine entered my head, and I momentarily felt my feet slip into space; then the vertical lines of the doors and windows twisted straight.

When I came back to the room, the drapes were open to a view of the apartment across the street and the downtown skyline above the roofs and the pale shapes of clouds in the sky. A few planes moved under the bellies of the clouds, like artificial stars or massive glowbugs. Nathan had cleared the table, except for the wine. He sat in the square stuffed chair. He fit in half, and his arms were pale and skeletal. His skull stood black in the halo of his thin hair, glowing in the lamplight. The tumbleweeds of his hands clawed the arm rests. I didn't want to make a pass at him.

"What's wrong?" I asked.

"I'm tired, that's all."

"Don't you like me?"

"Yes. It's not that."

"What are we not saying?" I asked him. But I had turned around and I didn't want him to answer. I just wanted to get all of the crap, him spitting out my spaghetti and his skull-like cheekbones, not necessarily on the table, but at least up toward the surface where we could look at it. I examined our reflection in the window, Nathan sitting on the chair and my hips a little too wide and a little too healthy. I didn't want to go home drunk to Mr. Paterson. "Won't you at least let me sleep in bed with you?"

He looked out the window. His head nodded into a clenched fist. It doubled like a knot in a thick rope. "Okay. But that's my limit."

"I'll accept that," I said.

"I mean it," he said.

We lay in his bed, small enough that my side, soft and fleshy, pressed into the hard, sharp angles of his body. But his skin was hot and still smelled like lavender. I listened to the sick rise of his breath. It rose into the cavity of his mouth, and hissed in the chambers of his lungs. I pulled the smooth shape of his head against my breasts, until the hiss settled, and his breath smoothed. I fell asleep to the quiet rhythm, looking forward to the gray light of the morning, when I could wake, me in bed with him and he in bed with me.

The Remains of River Names

———•———

Some mornings when I wake and look at you, I realize you haven't been having an easy time of it. Hair twists around your ears, your eyes fill with sticky sleep and your face wrinkles in thick, plastic folds. I only see you after I've swatted the brass alarm clock, as I iron my shirt and lower the legs of the ironing board as quietly as I can, lightly holding the thin aluminum legs the way I used to circle your wrist. You are almost always asleep, having just come home from the late shift at the Westward Inn Restaurant. You lie dreaming, your hands twisting the tops of the blankets into horns.

I realize that you could just get out of this situation, and get on with whatever real life you had planned for yourself before you met me. I hope that something besides the reflex of getting up and going to work, coming home and going to sleep, is holding you near me, something besides habit.

On one of our days off together, I ask you to tell me what you dream about while you sleep next to me. We sit in bed, drinking coffee from old white mugs you stole

183

from work. You lay back against the wall and tell me that you dream of great brown rivers flowing through thick jungles, and rocky mesas with orange lightning crackling through desert air, and rain falling with a hush on plains of long yellow grass. I know you've never been to places like these.

When I wake up, you lie next to me. Your slack lips press into the pillows that neither of us ever gets around to washing so that they are stained grey with weeks' worth of your make-up and my hair gel. You sometimes mutter things as I lean out of bed, my elbows on my knees and my head propped on my hands as I prepare for another day, at the end of which I will return to this room, drop my clothes and climb into this empty bed, while you finish with the ironing board and leave for work.

"What're you thinking?" you asked me on that day off together. And I lied. A person cannot say, "Blank, nothing." Instead I made something up. The more poetic the better, the more you believed it, not that I think you actually believed it, but you liked the sound of it, the way I like the sound of your dreams. I told you that I was imagining what you were dreaming. I imagined that you dreamed of a grove of sword ferns in the summer when the birds pull moss off the branches of the maple trees. I told you of your plains of long grass with a gentle wind rustling the blades and the undersides turning up so that they are silver. I will tell you anything that takes us away from the noise of traffic on the highway just outside our windows, from the arguing parents next door. What I was really thinking about was cutting my toenails, and playing out the process in my mind. Where are the toenail clippers? In the wicker basket on top of the toilet. I turn the handle of the clippers back into the ready position, lean over the toilet, my belly presses into my pelvis, making it ache slightly, while I cut the nails and let them fall into the porcelain bowl.

I do dream about you. I dream about being awake with you and we are driving in our car, the way it used to be before the wreck. We drive along the freeway for miles and miles, like my family used to do, in and out of nowhere, just you and me and the casual static of the FM dial.

The summer we met, the summer I was fifteen, Mom sent me to live with an old friend she knew from when she grew up in Snoqualmie. Joseph Anderson had sometimes baby-sat her and some of the other neighborhood kids. Mom said that he had always lived in his house and that he owned a big stretch of old farm land along the swamp where the North and Middle Forks of the Snoqualmie met. "He's a nice man," she said. "You'll like him, and it's just for a couple of months while I find real work and get a real place."

But already I didn't like the idea of going back to the Snoqualmie Valley where we had once lived with Dad and my brother. When I thought of the valley, I always thought of the smell of wood smoke and my unsuccessful chore of making the wood fire in the winter, in the morning before everyone else woke. I would lay the crinkled newspaper down, and spread the kindling out over it. Finally I would stuff in the logs I hoped would start burning. On the cast-iron stove, I would flick a match from the book Mom had picked up from the diner where she worked and set the paper on fire. I'd watch the paper burn and then the kindling turn white and the slightly blackened logs falling into the ashes. By this time Dad would've stumbled into the bathroom. He'd come out grumbling about my incompetence while he reset the fire. He'd squat down in front of the sooty mouth of the stove, holding me in the sweet, sweaty smell between his arms, to watch him set the fire. In seconds he'd have a blaze going. "Watch and remember," he'd say on good mornings. On bad mornings he'd tell me I was just plain dumb and would wait until I got the thing started. Then my hands would shake so badly from thinking he would hit me that I would end up getting hit.

Mr. Anderson's house sat next to a small lake layered with lily pads and behind his house blackberry tangles and stands of pine trees grew where fields had once been. The house itself barely held up its roof. The moss-covered shingles sagged in the middle of the house like a huge, soaked hat. An old man stood on the porch in a pair of overalls and he smiled and held his arms apart for Mom to put herself in-between. He laughed and it sounded like he was saying "Ho ho ho" over and over again. His head had started to lose hair, not like balding but more like molting. Patches of pinkish skin showed through his hair. His wrinkles folded so deep I thought that if I unraveled them he would fold out flat like an uncrumpled ball of paper. He nodded solemnly to me and took my hand and gripped it so hard that I wanted to scream. I also wanted to laugh because I wondered how much effort it was taking him to get this kind of grip working. "Dillon, it is a pleasure to meet you. Your mother has talked all about you." He looked at Mom and wagged his head. He laughed again, "Ho ho ho."

"Let's go inside," he said. He probably was one of those good looking guys when he was young—the movie star among his friends—a long angular jaw and light brown hair and his height. But he stood with a crooked stoop now, teetering to one side and then the other as he tried to grab my two suitcases. I stepped in front of him and picked them both up. Before Mom could get a solid grip on hers, he grabbed the plastic handle and nodded at her. He followed us up the stairs. At the top of the stairs his face had turned red and a bluish vein like the inside part of a leaf filled up his forehead. He set Mom's suitcase on the top step and opened the front door. The porch looked like the porches I avoided when I used to trick or treat. Spiderwebs clung to the corners. Yellow newspaper, torn grocery bags, and empty plastic milk gallons filled the nook.

The house smelled like bleach and rose petals, smells I now associate with the old man's voice, an almost whisper that rose at the end of his sentences and paused to laugh. "Let's take a load off and get something to drink," he said. And then he laughed. My eyes started to adjust to the room. I closed the door behind me. A lamp, its shade cracked, let light through in jagged crevices of light. A TV sat in one corner, one of the old ones, in a big wooden cabinet and green plastic around the lip of the screen.

While we sat in the living room waiting for Joseph to return, Mom turned to me and squeezed my knee. "Isn't this great? You're back in the valley, and you can swim in the river and go hiking any time you want."

"Yeah, this is just great," I said.

Joseph returned with two cups of coffee on a tray and a can of a soft drink I had never seen before. It had old time letters and a green can.

"What is this?" I said.

"A local soda," Joseph said. "You can still get them in the Deli Mart in Snoqualmie. You'll like it."

It tasted like carbonated maple syrup. "I'm going to take the bags to my room, okay?"

"Upstairs," Joseph said. "I can show you the room."

"It's all right," I said.

I found my bedroom at the top of the stairway, an almost empty room, with wooden floors and old furniture someone had once painted white. The mattress was overstuffed. I slid my suitcases under the bed, hoping I would be able to just pull them out and leave when Mom was finished visiting with the old man.

When I came downstairs, I began to realize just how dusty and messed up this place was. "It'll be spotless by the end of the summer," Mom said to Joseph. "And then you can just hire a maid to come in once in a while. Thank you so much for taking him."

The next morning, Joseph started in with, "How much of the world have you seen, son?"

"Some," I said. "My Mom and Dad used to drive around a lot."

"I've knocked around a bit. Have you eaten breakfast?" he asked me. He asked me again when I didn't respond. I was afraid to say no, because I didn't understand how I should treat this man who I suddenly had to live with and work for. "I haven't had anything to eat," I said. Joseph stood like a papier-maché marionette, brittle and frail, and shuffled into the kitchen.

The kitchen was clean in that rotting food didn't lay out on the counter. Hundreds of knife gashes tarnished the formica counter top. In some places, so many scars crossed that the flecked gold and marbled pattern of the formica gave way to the plywood underneath. Splattered grease drops hardened behind the range; each drop looked like amber tree pitch. Rust coated the sink handles. Everything looked old, unmaintained, and over-used.

"Sit down and don't touch anything," Joseph said. I sat at the table in the dining nook. A tangle of blackberry vines pressed against the windows. Once they must have overlooked a pasture, the distant river, and the mountains.

"Quite a view," I said.

"Smart," Joseph said. "Your Mom teach you that?"

"I don't think so." I smiled because I supposed that she had. I didn't understand why she had sent me out here to be with this old man who couldn't take care of himself, much less take care of me. He stood at the counter working a can opener. "Back in my day, we beat a sense of respect, manners, and civility into our children."

"You mean, back in the day when you could stand up straight?"

"I still have enough of my spine to whip a whelp like you under the table. So you watch your mouth, son."

"You need help with that can opener?"

"I can manage," he said.

"Suppose anyone ever cut those vines back?"

"The vines aren't my fault. It's a cat's fault." Joseph dumped the tuna into a glass bowl and spooned in a jiggling heap of mayonnaise. "When you cut those vines down, you've got to watch your back. The cat's in there."

"What do you mean, when I cut down?" I asked. "Why would I do that?"

"It needs to be done."

"When am I going to do that?"

"Soon," Joseph said. "A woman who used to own the cat a long time ago had a garden next door. The woman was afraid of insects, in particular spiders."

"Spiders aren't insects," I said.

"They're bugs. That's enough," Joseph said. He spread the tuna onto slices of bread. "The cat used to hunt down and kill gardener snakes, leaving their bodies on my porch. They looked like piles of raw bacon."

Joseph set the sandwich on the table. The tuna paste dripped down the sides of the bread. He sat across from me in the dark recess of the dining nook. Through the window I could faintly see the sky through the thicket of crossing vines. "What's wrong? You don't like your food?"

"It's good," I said. But I didn't touch the sandwich, which had been on the formica counter.

"Eat your sandwich," Joseph said.

I bit off a hunk of the sandwich and started to chew. "This cat? It's dead now?"

"No, it's in there still. As you know, gardener snakes eat spiders. So before the woman brought the cat here, the fields from here to the Snoqualmie were full of snakes. You couldn't find any spiders. I didn't see a web in a long time. After the woman found the cat, our windows started to fill with spider webs. Spiders draped my roses with webs and in the spring black blooms of spiders crawled everywhere. I had to stop working in the greenhouse. The woman stopped working in her garden. Her blackberries, which she had kept for making jam, exploded and covered everything. I still have her jam somewhere."

"They exploded?"

He laughed, "Ho ho ho," and then said, "No. A figure of speech. It took a few years for the vines to grow."

I finished choking down my sandwich.

"You want another?"

"Thank you, no."

"I should have done something about those vines," Joseph said. "But they covered everything. And now it's going to take real work to cut them down. I regret I haven't done anything about those vines. Now it's too late. Too many years have gone by without me doing anything. If only I had remembered. You, as a young man, shouldn't let things like that happen."

Sometimes, after Joseph stopped reading the paper and had folded it up neatly on the table, he'd say, "It's all flash and mirrors, son." But he could have used a mirror and some serious light to see what kind of conditions he lived in. I spent that week cleaning up Joseph's house. Every night, I would go to my room and read and think that when Mom came this weekend I would make her take me back to Seattle and I would do anything except become a janitor.

I had to clean his bathroom. I told myself I would never have to do it again. I held my mouth open tasting, instead of smelling, the damp splotches of mold coating his ceiling. His tub, a real ancient model with a suspended belly and large talon claws pressed into the floor, lay under a grey crust that caked the sides like mud. Grit collected between the cast iron fingers. Where the shower curtain draped into the tub it had pasted to the muck.

The windows were sealed behind dirt, cob webs, and a light coating of moss. The place smelled like a forgotten port-a-potty. A thick chemical stench rose through the organic odor of decay. The room stunk. Even as I scrubbed out the medicine chest and found such important points of contact between the bathroom and the old man as his toothbrush—a faded plastic stick with a mess of fibers at one end like a miniature mop—I couldn't believe that he lived there. I couldn't believe that something human used the room.

I started with the bleach and opened the window. I left the door open, ripped the shower curtain down, and began. In an hour I had found the original white tile. In two hours, the room sparkled. It glowed, except for the sink faucet where the metal had rusted into rough brown knobs.

Joseph looked at the bathroom. I could tell he liked what he saw, but he stood by the window, letting the light and air fall over his wrinkled grey face. He didn't smile at me but he nodded his head. His eyes were filmed over like soap bubbles. "This is good, Dillon," he said to me like a concession; he conceded that his bathroom had been really so bad and once he had been able to keep it looking clean without anyone's help, but now he needed someone to help him.

On Friday, Mom called and said that she wouldn't be able to drive out that weekend. "I'm sorry, honey," she said. I decided to run away the next day. That is when I ran into you.

Would you have been interested in me then if you knew what you know now?

The night the accident happened, I didn't mean to drink anything at the Westward Inn. I had been at home all afternoon, drinking a little beer, and I was a little drunk when I came in early to pick you up and then you were able to give me the beers for free from the lounge so I started drinking them like I was stealing something.

I sat at the table, watching you circle the floor, talking to the customers, and then I had drunk a full glass and another one. When we finally went out to the car I had trouble fitting the key into the lock. You sat next to me and lay your head back on the seat. "I will sleep for a thousand years," you said. I thought that was so funny that I laughed until my throat hurt.

"Geez," you said. "It wasn't that funny."

When I ran the red light at the first intersection you should have stopped the car. I don't blame you, but you should have seen that I was having trouble keeping the car in between the yellow line and the white line. Instead you just said, "What was that?"

"A stale yellow."

"Looked like a red to me."

"It just turned," I said. You lay your head back and told me to wake you up when we got home.

And then we began the long drive on the highway and that's when I started missing seconds. The car suddenly drifted across the white line. One second an exit sign was a mile away and the next instant we were passing it. Things began to speed up that way. I had trouble keeping everything in order and then I was trying to stop us or steer our car out of the way of a blue Toyota. Our car smashed their car into the ditch and we swerved out back into our lane.

"What! What just happened?" You held onto your seat belt and stared into the darkness in front of us.

"I just hit a car," I said. "I must be more tired than I thought."

A police car was by the Toyota when we walked back. I had the car keys in my hands. They found me drunk. They found me guilty. Now instead of working for ourselves, we work to pay off these people.

That summer Saturday, years ago, while Joseph slept on the porch, I walked down the street and then started to run. I came to the bridge over the Snoqualmie. You and two boys about my age were swimming and jumping off the bridge.

Quickly I ran past, but I heard the three of you peel after me; your feet flopped on the pavement and your heels echoed in the trees. A stand of tall firs stood between a row of houses and the river. We ran, and I came to the end of the bridge and slid under the road so that you'd run over the bridge like a Warner Brothers' cartoon.

But you guys followed me under the bridge and we

circled one another, panting. The river slurped behind us. "Hi," your tall friend said. Blond hair wisped around his ears. His face was angular and his Adam's apple throbbed up and down. A head shorter, the other kid looked like a construction crew guy, a living Tonka Truck driver; his arms bulged. You slid down the bank and threw the hair out of your eyes and laughed at me.

Mr. Tonka didn't even breathe hard. "Hi, name is Keith." He gripped my hand as hard as possible and shook. "Call him Dayle. The girl's Valerie. Are you running away?"

"Where are you running away to?" you asked. "How're you going to eat?"

"He can fish," Keith said.

"It won't work," you said. "But I know what we can do. The real plan is that you don't want to live at home anymore, right? If we can do that you'll be happy?" You turned around. Behind you, the cement support of the bridge was covered with graffiti, Alice Cooper, Kiss, Pink Floyd Rocks. An old kitchen chair sat in one corner and a gutted fire pit took up the middle of the space. "You can live here. Keith and I can bring you extra food after dinner. I can bring you cereal in the morning."

"The underworld lies herein," Dayle said in a deep voice like he was quoting something, although I couldn't tell what.

"It'll be cool," Keith said. "I can come visit you and we can sit around in our cave and go out, like bandits, and terrorize the countryside."

We ended playing together all that day and I returned home and never did spend a night under the bridge.

At the bottom of the stairs in Joseph's house, the door to the bathroom sometimes swung open, especially if there was a window open in the living room. In the morning, I came down the stairs and stopped on the stairwell because I could see past the bathroom door to the vanity mirror where Joseph's reflection was. He stood at the sink with his face covered in white foam. He leaned over the sink, grasping the white porcelain rim of the bowl with one hand while he used a straight razor to scrape off the silver specks of his beard. He leaned back and lifted his chin and used one hand to smooth his wrinkles while he drew the sharp blade across the whiskers. A scraping noise filled the hallway. When he had finished, he rinsed the razor and put it away in a leather case and then washed his chin by setting his face in the basin and running steaming water over his head. He lifted his skull up and bumped it against the faucet. He grunted, a noise full of phlegm that came from deep in his throat. And then he caught sight of himself in the mirror. He squinted and then smiled, turning his profile just barely to one side and the next. He took a palmful of oil and slicked back his hair and smiled at himself, showing all of his teeth. Then he looked at me sitting on the stairs. "Good morning," he said.

"Hey," I said and rushed down the last of the steps and stood in the kitchen. The sight of him caring for himself, as if his appearance mattered, made me wonder how he saw himself. The picture of him in his army uniform by the fireplace was of a young man, a man younger than my brother Milton. I wondered how many years he had been in this house and why he was satisfied to just sit on his porch and read the newspaper.

"Fine morning." Joseph came into the kitchen. As I watched him open the cupboards and lay out the bowls for the oatmeal, one for him and one for me, I thought that I should help Joseph get his yard back to the way it had been. At that moment I felt sorry for the old man, not just because he had to pull apart his sagging skin to cut his whiskers, but because it seemed everything in his life had gone beyond his control. He couldn't even fight the easy battle of keeping weeds and blackberries out of his yard. I don't think he had a chance, in the long run, of keeping the whiskers off his face. One of the things I knew from my Mom's murder mysteries was how dead men's toenails and hair kept growing after death.

Over my oatmeal, slathered with butter and milk, I asked Joseph, "So you suppose you can give me a hand cutting down the blackberries behind your house?"

"The weather report says it's going to be a hot day," Joseph said.

"So you'll be able to help me?"

"I don't know. If it's hot out there I don't think it's a good idea."

"But I'll be starting in about ten minutes. Help me for an hour, before it gets hot."

"You want me to help?"

"Yes."

"Sure," he said. He smiled then. "I can make my old bones do some work." He laughed.

The sun had come over Mount Si when we started on the vines behind his house. They rose up in huge heaps. I began by cutting at the wall of berries. I tossed the leaves and thorns behind me while Joseph pulled them into a pile that we would burn later. We had been working for about twenty minutes, when I heard Joseph make a noise like he just had the wind knocked out him. I turned around and found him laying on the ground. He kneeled up onto one knee. "Do you need help?" I asked.

"No, I'm fine." He dusted off his knees. "That's it," he said. "I'm done for the day."

"Don't you want to help get your yard in shape?"

"It'll just grow back," he said.

"No, it won't."

"I'll get you some juice to drink," he said, and started walking back to the house.

Because I felt sorry for him, I let him go back to the house and I started back on the vines. As I got into the rhythm of cutting I forgot about Joseph and started to think about the cat prowling under the thickets of blackberries behind the place. The thought of what lay hidden in the bushes—old things, cast-off washing machines maybe, perhaps an ancient car—made me curious. Something was there, I thought, and I wanted to pull the vines down like a huge curtain to reveal whatever lay back there.

As I crashed into the thickets, watching for the cat and the spiders, I cut through the green shoots to the brittle gray vines hardened into a stick forest. Animal trails pushed through the underbrush. Hard pellets of rabbit droppings and bits of fur littered the worn paths. Above me, the arch of live vines formed a green roof. I cut at the foundations, making leaves flutter down.

I saw a small building at the edge of Joseph's yard, and then I heard something snarl. From the darkness a cat jumped onto me; its claws slashed my shirt. Its breath smelled acidic like rotting lard. I ripped the bottom of my shirt up, and captured the cat in the reverse bag of my shirt. The cat struggled in the makeshift net. I tossed the animal away, and the vines snapped like bones in its crash descent. I recovered the rags of my T-shirt. The cotton soothed my trickling wounds.

I cut the bushes aside and came to the small greenhouse at the edge of Joseph's yard. The glass roof pressed against the ceiling of blackberry leaves.

Streaming through the dirty panes, sunlight caught dust in the small space and made the air glow. The smell of fungus and mold hung in the air. Nothing had been touched for as long as it took the thicket outside to grow. I had broken the seal, like an Egyptian tomb, to the old greenhouse. I held my breath when I realized this, afraid, and then laughing at myself as I thought about the mummy's curse, and remembered how all of the explorers who had discovered King Tutankhamen had died bizarre deaths.

An old desk sat on a wooden platform in the far corner of the shed. I pushed through the plants, collapsing them into piles of dirt.

On the desk, a dusty framed picture of a woman stood out among the ancient clutter of empty pots and stacks of birthday cards held together with twine. The photograph was smudged and grainy. The woman, dark hair, black dots of serious eyes, stared at me. Not out of the photograph, but at me the boy who held the slightly rusted frame in his hand. I had seen girls look at me like this before, and in a few weeks I would welcome your look at the bridge, when you asked me, "Got a cigarette I could bum off you?"

Under the picture, someone had stuffed another one of the same woman leaning against a man in an Army uniform. I recognized Joseph by his long forehead and sharp nose, even through his hair was full. He wore a pair of tall boots that caught the sunlight in the bright photograph. Everything was almost silver. Behind him, I could see the arc of the mountains down to the water of the slough. But cattle grazed in the field right up to the edge of the water. He didn't look at the photographer, but over whoever took the picture, up into the sky or the treeline or wherever. He didn't lean slightly away from Ellen like he did now with me as if he expected me to knock him over. This man stood on the damp grass—you could see it was mushy with crab grass and cattails leaning out of the ditches—with his legs shoulder-width and planted so that no one could knock him over. His head was cocked slightly toward the women, Ellen Miller. Her body pushed right up next to him and his arm was around her. Her head was turned like she was drawn to the sound of someone calling from a long way off.

In the desk, I found a stack of papers folded together and tied with a piece of garden twine. The top papers, powdered with a light green dust, puffed onto my hands as I picked up the packet. I untied the string, and the papers came loose in my hand as brittle as a piece of shale unfolding. The top sheets crumbled; the green mold held the bottom sheets together, but their edges cracked, and damp paper flitted onto the dusty ground. The handwriting sloped long and slanted, like the writing in *The Constitution*.

September 26, 1948
Amherst, Massachusetts

Dearest Joseph,

I remember you. I dream about you almost every night, and the nights I don't, I am falling asleep wishing to dream about you—I don't sleep at all. I remember you every night.

199

I often daydream about what we could do next summer. I lie to myself about how long the school year will be—it won't be long, will it?

I have told my friends about you. I often think about the slough and your house there. You won't move, will you? I remember the reflection of the moon in the water, and you rolling through the dark water splashing and gurgling and making all of that noise. I dream I'm dipping my tongue in the pitted dimples of the moon. I remember your arms, and I remember what you never said to me. In fact, I remember all the things that were never said. I have things on my mind lately about you and problems about you that have been difficult to solve. But things have happened and maybe I will come home next summer and make you some blackberry pie.

Love Always,
Ellen Miller

———•———

October 20, 1948
Amherst, Massachusetts

Dearest Joseph,

I don't know if you received my first letter. I think about you often. Do you think about me?

School is starting to become busy, and I don't have time to do anything. By the weekends I'm exhausted.

Do you remember when we swam at midnight in the Snoqualmie River? I left my bracelet on the snag near your house. I just remembered this the other night as I was falling asleep and thinking about the smell of the river, that mix of mud and wood smoke. It'll be winter soon and then spring and the floods will come, so I guess the bracelet will be gone.

Please write.

Yours Truly,
Ellen Miller

———•———

October 30, 1948
Amherst, Massachusetts

Dearest Joseph,

I wrote my mother and she said that you are very busy. I find that hard to believe, considering. I just wrote to let you know I will always remember what your face looked like under the moon. The term ends soon, and I will be back for Thanksgiving. I hope to see you then.

It's almost Halloween. I'm trying to carve a pumpkin to look like you. I made the eyes right. It's the mouth that will be tricky.

Thinking of You,
Ellen Miller

I held the thin, frail paper in my hand and I thought that the letters were older than my mother, older than anyone I knew except the man who I worked for. With the letters, the photograph of the woman became complete. I saw her looking at whoever took the photograph; thinking that she needed to be as persuasive as possible, the photo would be going to Joseph. It would sit on his desk. It was all she had to lure him to her. This was the scenario I believed.

I began to see the girls my age differently. When my brother, Milton, had taught me how the parts of a car came together to run, how the engine broke the gasoline down, where the oil flowed, what the pieces did, the mysterious solid body of the car broke down into completely understood sections. I somehow learned something about one of the parts of women with the photograph, the letters, and a desire for Ellen that was not based on her physical presence or image but on the ghost of her presence that I found in these forgotten letters.

I raked leaves into a huge pile in the front of Joseph's yard, and I watched for the cat to lumber out of the brambles. I watched for anything to make Joseph's story real. After I had raked the leaves into a pile, I heaped them onto my arms, feeling their brittle edges and musty odor rush over my face, and I dumped them into an old oil drum. I burned the leaves. The smoke plume spiraled into the sky.

At dinner that night, while Joseph and I sat at the table, I asked him if he had ever been married. I watched him; I wanted him to think about Ellen, for his face to flush red and smooth.

"How come you didn't marry Ellen Miller?"

"Who?" Joseph asked and I could see that he didn't remember. He nodded his head. His hair was thin and wispy. It looked like the fungus in the earth of the greenhouse, slowly eating away the nutrients in the rotting mass of dead plants. The mold had even reached the pages of

Ellen Miller and she was gone from memory. I would not live like this. I vowed this then, and maybe that's the reason I think about Joseph now, because in the morning when I think about our isolation, how we are always sleeping when we see each other, I think that his life has become my life.

I threw the letters on the table and the photographs slid out, face down. Joseph picked up everything, and I saw his forehead tighten like it had when he tried to lug my mother's heavy suitcase inside. He read the letters, holding the paper in his liver-spotted hand. The edge of the paper shook. He finally said, "These letters are old." He looked at me and I stared into the blue rim of his eyes. But I couldn't tell what he was thinking.

"I have always been embarrassed by myself as a young man," he said. "I don't think of that young man as real now. He's more of a memory, and nothing else. He's an abstraction, like the word 'sacred' or 'sacrifice,' or the expression 'in vain.' You might recall they called that war I fought in, The Good War. I haven't seen anything good or sacred in things that require sacrifice. It's more like a salmon boat full of steelhead someone just dumps on the pier for the gulls and the flies. A waste of life. There are many words that I can't stand to hear, youth and promise and sacrifice being some of them. It's all, just about any word, really, smoke and flash and mirrors. Only the old names of places have dignity—they are the only spoken thing that is not a lie. Abstract words like sacrifice or hallow are barren beside the concrete names of rivers and mountains like Snoqualmie, Snohomish, Tahoma, and Klickitat."

"Did you find that in a book?"

"All of life is a book when it's said and done. And then

it's held in these grotesque words or these ridiculous photographs. You think this is photographic evidence? You think I remember these boots?"

"What about her?"

"This woman? I remember her, I think. I remember all of my women, one way or the other."

"What about the letters? These mean something, don't they?"

"These letters sum up how she and I knew each other like the name of the Snoqualmie tells you that there were once people who lived on the banks of this river and had a way of life that depended on the salmon that once made their way up this river. Time has dragged down the particulars of these people. Time has taken them away and time has taken whoever this girl was away."

He stood up. "I don't want to remember her."

I realized I had felt a sort of pity for this man who lived like an old rat in his falling-down house, but now I saw some of what he must see in the decaying fields and the falling roof. Maybe he wanted everything to be dragged down by the braids of blackberry vines. He wanted the weeds to grow up over the house so that everything would be gone.

I don't have a table at the Westward Inn, although I always sit in your section with my back to the window. You've teased me about my rituals, and this is one that I always hear from you. I come, after the last rerun of M*A*S*H, after the dinner rush has trickled out of the restaurant and the after-movie rush hasn't started to pour in. The floor is still a mess from dinner—fries lay squished in the carpet, shredded napkins under tables, crumbs and water glasses with napkins jammed in the top cover table tops. I sit down at an unbussed table and if you're too busy, Rance, the bus boy drops a cup of coffee at my table with a handful of Equal.

As I watch you work, I think of myself as a stranger, which by now I virtually am, and the tired, erotic cliché of taking you the waitress home after her shift and screwing her... The fact is we are always too tired. I come home and sleep and you brush your teeth and take a quick shower. I know you're back in bed because of the fat-fryer-and-smoking-section odor that never leaves your skin.

I want you to know I will see you awake again. I am not Joseph Anderson and I will not let you wander away like Ellen Miller or like some forgotten vocabulary question. You are not just a word or a name. And while this dreadful business of living, working, and sleeping makes us prisoners right now, I want you to know I will see you awake again. I am not Joseph Anderson.

Right now I don't even see you awake. I just see you sleeping. I imagine sometimes, when I'm looking at you, that we will both wake and walk together through the lands of your dreams, along a trail, say, next to a muddy river in the jungle, and we will come to a small, whitewashed, clapboard house with dirt floors. We will live in the house by the river, falling asleep as the dusk falls like rain into night.

Matt Briggs was born in Seattle in 1970. He was raised thirty miles east of Seattle in the Snoqualmie Valley by working-class, hippie parents. During the Gulf War, he served in Riyadh, Saudia Arabia as an army laboratory technician running urine analysis on canine units and prisoners of war. He graduated from the University of Washington in 1995 with a B.A. in English. He lives in Seattle with his wife, Lisa Purdy. His stories have appeared in *The North Atlantic Review*, *The Raven Chronicles*, *The Northwest Review*, and *ZYZZYVA*.